The Quilt Shop
in
KERRY
SPRINGS

Where dreams are stitched…patch by patch!

Welcome to the Blind Stitch quilt shop!
On Main Street, in the small town of
Kerry Springs, this is a haven where women,
young and old, gather to work on their quilts
and share their hopes and dreams.…

And they have much to wish for, because Kerry Springs is
home to some of the most deliciously brooding heroes in
the whole of Texas state!

Open one of Patricia Thayer's stories to enjoy the warmth
of a very special town and the strength of old-fashioned
community spirit. Best of all,
watch as Kerry Springs' singletons find
the love they deserve.…

Don't miss any of the books in this series:

Little Cowgirl Needs a Mom
August 2011

The Lonesome Rancher
September 2011

Tall, Dark, Texas Ranger
October 2011

Only from Harlequin Romance®!

Dear Reader,

I'm back in Kerry Springs. There are so many wonderful characters in this small Texas town, and this time I got to add a little danger, a little suspense, then throw in a sexy Texas Ranger and you have a great mix.

My heroine is Lilly Perry. You've met her briefly in *Little Cowgirl Needs a Mom*. She's the elementary school principal and a divorced mother with two kids, Kasey and Robbie. She has moved back into her childhood home with her widowed mother.

The twist is Ranger Noah "Coop" Cooper is working undercover. One day Coop comes knocking at her door, wanting to rent the cottage out back. Soon, he becomes the new handyman, doing repairs on the old Victorian home while trying to learn the truth about Lilly's ex-husband's death.

Even though Lilly has sworn off men, seeing this fine specimen shirtless, and with a tool belt slung low on his hips, causes her to reevaluate that decision—until she discovers it's all a lie.

I hope you enjoy their journey as much as I did writing the story.

Patricia Thayer

PATRICIA THAYER

Tall, Dark, Texas Ranger

The Quilt Shop in KERRY SPRINGS

TORONTO NEW YORK LONDON
AMSTERDAM PARIS SYDNEY HAMBURG
STOCKHOLM ATHENS TOKYO MILAN MADRID
PRAGUE WARSAW BUDAPEST AUCKLAND

Recycling programs
for this product may
not exist in your area.

ISBN-13: 978-0-373-17757-8

TALL, DARK, TEXAS RANGER

First North American Publication 2011

Copyright © 2011 by Patricia Wright

Patricia Thayer is the second of eight children and was originally born and raised in Muncie, Indiana. She attended Ball State University, and soon afterward headed West. Over the years she's made frequent visits back to the Midwest, trying to keep up with her growing family.

Patricia has called Orange County, California, home for many years. She not only enjoys the warm climate, but also the company and support of other published authors in the local writers' organization. For the past eighteen years she has had the unwavering support and encouragement of her critique group. It's a sisterhood like no other.

When she's not working on a story, you might find her traveling the United States and Europe, taking in the scenery and doing story research accompanied by Steve, her husband for more than thirty-five years. Together they have three grown sons and four grandsons. She calls them her own true-life heroes. On the rare days she's not writing, you might catch Patricia at Disneyland, spoiling those grandkids rotten! She also volunteers for the Grandparent Autism Network.

Patricia has written for more than twenty years and has authored more than thirty-six books for Harlequin. She has been nominated for both the National Readers' Choice Award and the prestigious RITA® Award. Her book *Nothing Short of a Miracle* won an *RT Book Reviews* Reviewers' Choice Award.

A longtime member of Romance Writers of America, she has served as president and has held many other board positions for her local chapter in Orange County. She's a firm believer in giving back.

Check her website at www.patriciathayer.com for upcoming books.

To Mom,
Your strength and endurance amazes me.
I'm one proud daughter.

CHAPTER ONE

COULD this be his lucky day?

Noah Cooper drove down Maple Street and saw the Cottage For Rent sign in the front yard of the three-story Victorian house. He couldn't get any closer if he'd planned it. Now all he had to do was make sure he became the new tenant. He parked his truck at the curb under the large tree and climbed out, immediately feeling the Texas heat.

He also felt a stir of excitement as he made his way up the walk to the porch and climbed the crumbling concrete steps to the peeling porch floor and rang the bell.

It was a new job. A new challenge.

No answer. He glanced down and saw the sign on the doorknob that read, Gone Quilting.

Not to be detoured, he followed the wraparound porch to a set of stairs and a pathway that led to a large backyard. Even though the house looked a little shabby there were colorful flowers that filled the beds and the lawn had been recently cut. He guessed it paid to have family in the landscaping business.

In the back of the large lot he spotted a second structure. It was a much smaller scale, but the cottage was a single-story clapboard with decorative shutters. The same gray and burgundy colors that were faded and peeling as the main house. Even though it might be a little feminine for his tastes, the location was ideal. He started for the door, hoping to get a look inside.

Stepping up onto the small porch, he saw the door ajar and heard music. Peering inside, he found a main living area with a brick fireplace. On the other wall was a row of cabinets with compact appliances and a small table with two chairs. The place was furnished, but from what era? That was when he spotted the movement.

A woman was on her hands and knees scrubbing the floor, keeping in time with the country song. Her nice shapely bottom swaying back and forth as her arms fought against the dirty tile, singing along with Carrie Underwood. Rich brown hair with golden strands was pulled up in a knot on top of her head, but most had escaped. Her tank top and shorts showed off a trim but curvy body.

His body suddenly came alive. In his profession that didn't happen often, especially in the past year. But now wasn't the time to suddenly get his libido back. He had a job to do.

"Excuse me, ma'am," he called over the music.

Lilly heard her name and looked over her shoulder to find the stranger. She jumped, nearly hitting her head on the table.

She swore softly and the man started toward her. Holding up her hand, she stopped him from coming too close.

"Are you all right?"

With a nod, she managed to get to her feet and shut off the music. Then she turned around to get a look at her intruder.

Big. Tall. He had nearly black hair, thick and wavy, but his eyes were a whiskey-brown. He was dressed in faded jeans and a chambray shirt and boots much like south Texans, but she'd grown suspicious of any strangers.

"Who are you?" she said a little too harshly.

He didn't look to be intimidated at all. "I'm hoping I'll be your new tenant," the man said with a nod of his head. "I'm Noah Cooper."

"Lilly Perry, but I'm not the landlord. It's my mother, Beth Staley, who owns the place and she rents out this cottage." When her mother had decided to rent the cottage, they hadn't talked about who they'd rent to, but surely not a…stranger. "You'll have to come back."

"Do you know when that will be?"

Lilly felt an odd feeling go through her as the man continued to stare at her. As if those deep-set eyes could read her thoughts. "To be honest, Mr. Cooper—"

"It's Coop," he interrupted. "I go by Coop."

"Coop," she repeated. "I believe there's someone else interested in the place."

He nodded toward the door. "The sign is still up in the yard."

He'd got her there. "Well, it's not official. I'm just letting you know so you don't get too excited."

"I guess I need to come back and talk to Mrs. Staley then. When will she be back?"

Lilly shrugged. "It's hard to say, she's with her friends quilting. It could be hours."

He nodded, looking disappointed. "Okay. I guess I'll have to wait."

He turned to leave when she heard the familiar voice. "Mom! Mom! Where are you?"

"I'm in here, Robbie," she called and went to the door.

As fast as lightning, the five-year-old raced through the cottage door. "Colin and Cody are going swimming and they asked me to go, too. Can I, can I? Please."

"Robbie, slow down." She brushed back her son's blond hair that fell over his forehead. He stared back at her with blue eyes so like his father's. It still caused her chest to tighten at the memories of their previous life. A father he'd never know.

"If it's okay with Colin and Cody's mom?"

"Yeah, she said you could probably get some more work done without me underfoot."

She wanted to grin. Her son started talking at a year and hadn't slowed down since. "Maybe I should just put you to work, too."

He wrinkled his freckled nose. "Mom, I'm only five years old."

"Funny, yesterday you were counting the days to your sixth birthday."

"But I'm still a kid. I need to have some fun. It's summer vacation." Her son finally noticed Mr. Cooper. "Hi, who are you? I'm Robbie Perry."

"Robbie, this is Mr. Cooper," she said, keeping a protective hand on her child's shoulders.

"Everyone calls me Coop, Robbie."

Her son glanced at her, then back at the stranger. "What are you doing here with my mom?"

"Robbie." She hoped to send a warning by her tone. She wasn't happy with her son's attitude, even if he had cause to be suspicious.

"It's okay," Coop said. "He's looking out for his mother." He turned his attention to Robbie. "I want to rent this house. But your mother said someone else is interested in it."

Robbie's frown deepened. "There is? Who, Mom?"

Lilly felt her cheeks flame. Now her fib just got bigger. "I'm not sure." She quickly changed the subject. "Why don't you go and get your swim trunks and a towel."

His eyes widened. "I can go?"

Lilly didn't seem to have a choice. With her nod, her son did a fist pump and ran out.

"That's quite a boy you have there."

"Yes, he is. I wish I had his energy."

There was an uncomfortable silence, then Coop spoke. "Well, I should go, too," he said. "Thank you, Mrs. Perry."

"Sorry it didn't work out," she said. "Hope you find a place. Are you working in the area?" Why was she asking? "I mean the ranches might be hiring if you have some experience."

Coop could see Lilly Perry was leery of him. After everything that had happened in the past few months, of course she would be, especially of any strangers. "I have ranching experience, but that's not what I'm doing now. I'll be working on the new houses project on the west side of town."

He saw her surprise. "For AC Construction? You work for Alex Casali?"

"Yes, ma'am. I'm a finish carpenter by trade." That part wasn't a lie. If he pushed her for the cottage again, he might frighten her off. "Well, I guess I better continue my search. Goodbye."

Coop walked out the door, then along the path when the boy ran out of the main house. A bundle of energy, he bounded down the steps at full speed.

"Hey, Robbie," Coop called, wondering if the boy could help him. "Hey, by chance could you tell me where your grandmother has gone?"

He nodded. "Oh, yeah, she's quilting with her friends at the Blind Stitch." He rolled his eyes. "It's boring. They cut up old shirts and things to a make quilts. My sister does it, too."

"That's good because guys have things that are just for guys."

The boy looked thoughtful. "Yeah, but I don't get to do them too much 'cause my dad died."

"I'm sorry to hear that." He didn't know what to say to the kid. A horn honked and let him off the hook. "Have fun swimming."

Coop watched the boy run off to the waiting car. He silently cursed the man for what he'd done to this family. Michael Perry had a pretty wife and a couple of kids. He lost it all so quickly.

It was Coop's job to find out who was behind Perry's death. Was he the informant that never showed that night, or was it all just a coincidence?

Now, he planned on finding the truth, and preventing any other people getting hurt in the process.

Thirty minutes later, Coop found the Blind Stitch on Main Street. Not that it was that hard. The town of Kerry Springs, Texas, had a population of only about ten thousand. But he knew from experience that not all the people were good citizens.

He opened the door and walked inside. Okay, maybe he would be more comfortable going into a seedy bar in El Paso, but he had a job to do.

The store was laid out well. He was met with rows of colorful fabric that crowded the shelves and handmade quilts adorned the high walls. A large cutting table was busy with patrons waiting patiently for their turn. On the other side was a large doorway, opening into another area that had several rows of tables with sewing machines.

Finally a young blonde woman came up to him, her stomach round from the late stage of pregnancy.

"Hello, I'm Jenny Rafferty," she said. "Is there something I can help you with?"

"I was told that I'd find Beth Staley here."

The woman smiled. "Yes, Beth is here." She nodded to a round table in the corner in the front of the windows where half dozen women sat. "'The Quilting Corner' ladies."

He nodded. "Thank you, ma'am." He released a breath. He needed to sell this to make his job easier. Hat in hand, he put on a smile as he made his way to the table. The half dozen women, all different ages, suddenly stopped their conversation and stared at him.

"Good afternoon, ladies," he said. "I apologize for interrupting, but I'm looking for Mrs. Beth Staley."

"That would be me." A tiny woman in her late fifties raised her hand. "Are you sure you got the name right?"

The other woman laughed and Coop relaxed a little. "I'm sure if you're the woman who has the cottage for rent?"

When Beth smiled, he saw the resemblance to her daughter. Same sapphire eyes and shape of the face. The woman flashed a look at her friends, then back to him. "Why, yes, I do."

"Then I'm interested in renting it. I hope I'm not too late."

Mrs. Staley looked confused. "Why, Mr. Cooper, would that be?"

"Your daughter said there's another interested party."

Mrs. Staley sobered. "Oh, yeah, right. Well, that fell through so the cottage is still available. But, young man…"

"Sorry, it's Noah Cooper. Everyone calls me Coop."

"And I'm Beth, and these are my friends, Liz, Lisa, Millie, Louisa and Caitlin."

"It's a pleasure to meet you all."

They all returned greetings.

"Excuse us, ladies." Beth stood and moved away from the table for more privacy. "Well, Mr. Cooper, if you're serious about the cottage, I'll need references…and a deposit."

Coop nodded in agreement. "Not a problem. My new job is with AC Construction. But I can give previous references from San Antonio." His superiors wouldn't have any problem coming up with something.

"You're working for Alex?"

Coop nodded again. "Yes. I'm a finish carpenter by trade. I'd rather not live in a motel for the next six, or eight months." He'd had worse accommodations. "When I saw your cottage, it was a nice surprise." He needed to sweeten the deal. "And I've done a lot of home restoration work in the past, and I could help with some repairs around your beautiful home."

"I'm ashamed to say, my home has been neglected so badly. When my husband was alive he did all the repairs." She folded her arms over her chest covered by a shirt that said, I'd Rather Be Quilting. "Would you have the time to work on my place with your other job?"

"My job doesn't start for a few weeks. And I'm ready to move in right now. Of course, you need to check my references first."

She wrinkled her nose. "I figure if you work for Alex Casali, you must be top-notch. His wife, Allison, owns this shop."

"So Mrs. Casali quilts, too."

Beth grinned. "You could say that. She's one of the best." She motioned him back to the table. "Ladies, Noah Cooper is going to be my new tenant."

"Mother?"

Everyone turned to see Lilly Perry walking toward the

group. She'd cleaned up from earlier, and changed into a pair of khaki shorts and a pink T-shirt. Her brown hair was brushed and laying in soft waves against her shoulders. He'd never guess this woman was in her mid-thirties, and the mother of two.

"Mother, what's going on?"

"Good, Lilly, you're here. I want to introduce you to Mr. Cooper."

"We've already met," Lilly said, not looking happy. "He came by the house earlier." She stared at him. "How did you know to come here?"

"Your son, Robbie. He told me where to find Mrs. Staley. I didn't want to miss the opportunity. You said someone else was interested in it."

Beth looked at her daughter. "Who else?"

"Mandy Hews."

The older woman frowned. "She's only eighteen. Not only couldn't she afford it, but I'd spend all my time chasing off that boyfriend of hers. Good Lord, don't the women of this generation have any taste in men? The kid doesn't even have a job."

Lilly didn't like being called out in front of a stranger. "Excuse us, please." So she took her mother by the hand and pulled her away. Once across the room and out of earshot, she spoke. "Mother, you shouldn't have agreed to rent to this man before you checked him out. Besides, I thought we decided to rent to a woman."

"If I remember, you decided that. Besides, I wasn't born yesterday and I know how to size up people. Don't let your relationship with Michael cloud your judgment."

"Michael did a hell of a lot more than cloud my judgment. He kicked me and the kids to the curb and took every dime of our money. Not to mention he humiliated me."

Beth's expression softened. "I know, honey. And I wish

I could change that, but I can't. Don't you think it's time to move on? Start a new life for you and the kids."

Lilly did not want to rehash her problems right here in the Blind Stitch. There had been enough gossip about her around town to last a lifetime.

She glanced at the handsome Noah Cooper as he talked with the ladies around the table. He seemed to be very charming. That was the problem.

Mike had been charming when he wanted to be during their thirteen-year marriage. Then overnight things seemed to sour between them and he left her and the kids.

Suddenly there was a loud groan and everyone turned to Jenny who was doubled over. She gasped as a puddle formed on the floor below her.

She blushed. "Oh, God. My water broke."

The group got up and went to her.

"My baby's coming." Jenny sucked in a breath. "I've got to call Evan."

"I'll do it," Liz said to her. "You sit down."

Jenny shook her head. "No, I need to keep walking. I want this over quickly. Call Jade, see if she's on duty today. I want her in the delivery room."

Lilly watched as Jenny shouted orders, but everyone seemed confused. She'd had enough. She stuck her two little fingers in her mouth and whistled. The frenzy stopped.

"Okay, let's get organized here. Liz, you call Evan and tell him to meet us at the hospital. Millie, you phone Jade and let her know that Jenny's in labor, then get Jenny's phone and call her doctor to let her know she's on her way." She glanced around. "Now who brought their car?"

Silence. Then Noah Cooper spoke up. "I have my truck. It'll carry four people."

Jenny groaned with another contraction.

"Okay, Mr. Cooper," Lilly said. "You've been designated as official driver. Let's go people."

Lilly put her arm around Jenny and Liz took the other side and walked the expectant mother to the door. Her mother went with Coop to the door. "My daughter is a school principal," she told him. "She's good under fire."

"And she keeps a cool head," Coop said as he went outside, and he hurried to his truck at the curb. Opening the passenger side Millie placed a towel on the seat. Jenny apologized for making a mess.

"Not a problem, ma'am." He helped her in, then raced around the other side, took his duffel bag out of the backseat and tossed it in the pickup bed. He climbed in the driver's seat and started the engine. Lilly and her mother got in the back and gave directions to the hospital.

Lilly hoped to give up her supervisory position when they arrived. And the way Mr. Cooper was driving, it would be soon. She had to say one thing for the man: he hadn't run away when things got dicey. That was a point in his favor, but only one.

A little over two hours later, Noah was on his second cup of hospital coffee and still no baby. At least the father had arrived and was with his wife. He would have left but he wasn't sure how the rest of the women would get home. And it was his chance to get to know more townspeople.

He leaned against the wall and watched as so many people came in and out of the waiting area. It seemed Jenny Rafferty was well liked in this town. According to Beth, Jenny's husband, Evan Rafferty, was a local rancher/vineyard owner. The grandfather, Sean Rafferty, walked into the waiting area with his ten-year-old granddaughter, Jenny's stepdaughter, Gracie. Both were very excited about the upcoming arrival of the new addition to the family.

Sean Rafferty was the one who drew the women. They were swarming around the older gentleman as if he were a rockstar. Beth let it be known to him that Sean was the most eligible bachelor in town for their age group.

Coop's attention went to Lilly Perry who stood outside the sliding doors as she talked on her cell phone. She was probably checking on her kids. He recalled seeing her earlier, giving orders to everyone. She was a strong, take-charge woman. Was it possible she knew what had been going on? Had she known what her husband was involved in? Had that been the reason they split up?

Man, she'd be a hard woman to walk away from.

The door swished opened again and his new employer, Alex Casali, walked in with an attractive redhead he knew to be his wife, Allison Cole Casali.

Alex spotted him and excused himself. "Cooper, what are you doing here?"

"I just happened to be in the right place at the right time. I was the only one who had a vehicle close by to drive Jenny to the hospital."

Casali smiled. "Welcome to small-town living."

CHAPTER TWO

"It's a boy!"

Lilly looked up to see Evan Rafferty, dressed in hospital scrubs, in the waiting-room doorway. Several of the others in the group jumped up and offered their congratulations.

Sean was hugging his son when Lilly approached. "It's wonderful news, Evan."

The handsome new father grinned. "Yeah, it is. I wanted a boy, but another girl would have been great, too."

Lilly felt tears of joy, recalling the happiest days of her life had been when she had her children. "How is Jenny doing?"

"She's a champ," Evan said. "Not one complaint. Jade was with her, and I was her coach."

Lilly thought about her good friend. Jade was a nurse at the hospital and had recently married ranch owner Sloan Merrick. "I'm glad. How much did the baby weigh?"

"Sean Michael is eight pounds and six ounces."

Grandfather Sean appeared. "Did I hear right?"

Evan nodded. "Jenny wants our son to have a family connection so we thought what better way than his grand-father and great-grandfather's names? We thought we'd call him Mick."

Lilly could see that Sean was touched. The big burly man didn't have a problem showing his emotions as tears filled his eyes. "My dad would have liked that." Sean looked down at his granddaughter. "What do you think, Gracie? Doesn't that sound like a good Irish name?"

The ten-year-old nodded. "I like it. When can we see him, Dad? He *is* my brother."

The group laughed and Evan said, "Come on, I think family has some privileges."

Lilly watched as the threesome walked down the hall together. She felt envy for what she used to have, and had lost. What her kids had lost. Sadness engulfed her, but she refused to give in to it. She'd spent months trying to figure out what had happened with her marriage. What had happened between her and Mike. She never came up with any answers.

She shook off the sad thoughts, knowing she needed to get home. She turned toward the window and found Mr. Cooper leaning against a pillar.

She nearly groaned. Why was he still here? Well, she would soon find out as he started toward her.

"I take it everything's okay?"

She nodded, not wanting him to see that his presence bothered her. "A healthy baby is always the best news." She finally made eye contact with him. He did have great eyes. "You didn't need to hang around. I can get a ride back."

"Not a problem. I was hoping to find out when I can move into the cottage."

She still wasn't sure she wanted a stranger so close to her kids. "You'll have to ask my mother."

"I did, she said it depends on when you finish cleaning. Not that I can't finish the rest on my own."

"I was planning on cleaning the carpets. No one has lived in the place since my uncle stayed a few years back." She sucked in a breath and caught his scent. A tingle of awareness she hadn't felt in a long time went through her. She quickly got back on track. "Oh, and there are still some boxes I'll need to move into the garage. I haven't made the bed, and there aren't any towels."

The sound of his phone interrupted her rambling. He grabbed his cell off his belt, checked the number, shut it off, then looked back at her.

He seemed far too comfortable, while she couldn't even manage to put a sentence together. "I can move boxes and make a bed," he told her. "I have a few towels in my duffel. Tomorrow I can shop for whatever else I need. So when do I move in?"

Never! Lilly wanted to scream. She didn't need the complication, but for now they could use the extra income from renting the cottage. That was if she ever wanted to get out of debt. And thanks to her mother, she and the kids had a roof over their heads.

She glanced back at Mr. Cooper. "I guess now is fine."

He nodded and they started toward the exit, but she detoured and stopped by her mother first. "Are you ready to go home?"

Beth glanced past her daughter and saw Noah Cooper. "Well, I wanted to get a glimpse of little Mick. Why? Do you need something?"

"Mr. Cooper wants to move in right now. So I need to finish up a few things."

"Okay, I'll be home in about an hour." Her mother went to the new tenant. Lilly watched the two in conversation, then Beth came back smiling.

Great. Was she the only one who was suspicious of strangers?

Coop was careful not to push for conversation on the drive back to the Staley house. He already knew Lilly

Perry wasn't exactly happy to have him in the cottage. One wrong move and she would find an excuse to cut him loose. He needed to be here. It was a perfect place to possibly learn more about Delgado.

A long shot maybe, but it was the best he had.

Lilly instructed him to pull into the driveway and park on the far side of the garage. "There's enough room for all our vehicles."

"Thank you. That's a lot more convenient." He got out and grabbed his duffel from the truck bed.

He waited until Lilly came around and together they walked to the cottage. She took out a set of keys.

"I thought small towns were safe enough to leave your houses unlocked."

Coop watched a panicked look mar her pretty features. "It used to be that way. Things change."

From the information he had about Mike Perry's death, Lilly's home had been broken into. Shortly after that she'd lost the house to creditors and moved herself and the kids back here. Probably the safest place for her. But he wondered about that, too. Not with Delgado out there.

They walked inside. This time he took a better look at the rental. It was small, but homey and the furniture looked comfortable. He carried his bag into the other room where a queen-size bed took up most of the space.

He peered into the bath. A small shower stall and a pedestal sink and toilet were accounted for. "Everything I need," he said.

"There's a television, but only basic cable."

"That's more than I expected."

"Tell that to my kids. They seem to think they're deprived without the premiere channels."

"With you as their mother, and Beth as their grandmother, I'd say they're pretty lucky."

That seemed to frazzle her. "Well, having a mother who's the school principal doesn't exactly make them the most popular kids."

It beat the heck out of having a mother who didn't care about anything but the next man in her life. After two bad marriages, Cindy Morales was still looking for the elusive husband. That meant leaving her two boys alone. "They'll live," he said.

That comment got him a smile. "Well, I'll let you get settled in. Holler if you need anything."

"Wait." He pulled out his wallet and took out five one-hundred-dollar bills. "Here's part of the deposit. Tell your mother, I'll have a cashiers check for her in the morning."

Her eyes rounded as she stared down at the money.

"The banks are closed now."

She nodded and started for the door. He didn't want her to leave. That wasn't a good thing. He was here to do a job, nothing more. "I'd like to do some repairs around here," he called to her. "Will that bother you?"

She turned around. "You don't have to."

He shrugged. "I'll have some time before my job starts. Let's say my hobby is old Victorian homes."

She didn't look convinced. "I would think that you'd want to take advantage of the free time."

"I've had too much time off already. And I'll get to do something I love." That wasn't a lie. He did like to repair and refinish things.

"Well, Mother could use some help with the upkeep. It's really too big for her since my dad died, but she'll never leave here."

"It's a great house. And there seems to be plenty of room for you and your kids. I'm sure your mother likes having you all here with her."

She shrugged. "There wasn't a choice. We didn't have

anywhere else to go. Goodbye, Mr.—Coop." She turned and walked out.

This time Coop didn't stop her departure. He didn't want to scare her off for good. If he wanted to get any information, he needed to tread lightly.

His phone vibrated and he pulled it off his belt and checked the caller ID. It was his captain's private line, because they didn't want any of his calls traced back to the office.

"Coop here."

"How's it going?" Ben Collier asked.

"Fine, so far. I checked in with Casali yesterday." The lucrative rancher/businessman had hired him for the project with only the sheriff's request. No more details given. "He's awarded Perry's Landscaping the housing project job. I'm also renting a cottage at the Staley house."

"Good." There was a long pause. "I'd tell you not to take any unnecessary chances, but I know I would be wasting my breath. Since you're pretty much working on your own, just tread lightly around Delgado. If he gets wind of you nosing around, it could be dangerous for all involved. Outside of the local law enforcement, you have no partner as back up."

Coop's immediate concern was Lilly Perry and her family. "I'm good at my job."

"No one questions that, but you're personally involved."

His chest tightened as he thought about his half brother, Devin Morales. "We've got to get this guy off the streets."

"We will."

The connection was broken when Coop closed his phone. He knew firsthand that Raul Delgado was trouble. For years, he'd been involved with drug and weapons trafficking along the Mexico border. Yet, they couldn't link him to any of the killings or the thousands of pounds of illegal drugs coming into the U.S.

Even with the government's increased patrols, Delgado had managed to do business until one night a local cop was killed trying to break up a drug deal. Of course there were no witnesses to the crime. Coop fisted his hands, remembering how his younger brother Devin's life had ended too soon.

Yet, Delgado got away. Last word on the street was he'd relocated his operation from the El Paso area, possibly to Laredo.

Last year, he'd been tracked to Kerry Springs and to Perry's Landscaping. Four months ago, the Feds had received anonymous tips about Delgado's activity.

They'd set up a meeting with the informant at a secret location outside of town, but the guy never showed. A strange coincidence occurred when a partner in Perry's Landscaping, Mike Perry, committed suicide a few days later.

Coop strongly suspected Perry had some help with his death. No proof, yet. They weren't one hundred percent sure it had even been Perry who'd notified the authorities, either.

Coop thought about Lilly. Had she known what happened to her husband? Was that why she was leery of strangers?

Then he remembered the file on her. Mike and Lilly had been divorced for nearly a year by then. Had it been because of her husband's involvement with Delgado?

That was what he had to find out.

There were only two leads. Lilly's ex-sister-in-law, Stephanie Perry, was involved with a man named Rey Santos who looked remarkably like Raul Delgado. And the informant had told the Federal agents he had proof of Delgado's illegal activity.

Now all Coop needed to do was keep the promise he made at his brother's gravesite to catch this bastard while keeping the fact that he was a Texas Ranger a secret. Not too hard.

"Mom, Robbie's being gross again," thirteen-year-old Kasey Perry yelled from the top of the stairs.

Lilly sighed. It had been a long day already. She'd only walked in the door and hadn't even put down her grocery bags.

"Get washed up so we can eat."

"But, Mom, aren't you going to do something?"

Lilly leaned against the open banister and said, "I'll talk to him."

She headed down the hall ignoring any and all comments from the kids. Inside the big homey kitchen, she found her mother sitting at the counter, sipping a cup of coffee.

This room was Beth's space. Cabinets lined the walls and the tiled countertops were still in good shape and an island provided a good work space.

Beth Staley loved to cook and this big old kitchen had seen a lot activity over the years. Not so much lately. At least the table was set and ready for food. It was Lilly's turn to cook, but she wasn't ready.

"Give me a few minutes."

"There's no hurry," her mother said. "Just make a salad. We're having the rest delivered."

"Mother," she warned as she started to empty the grocery bag. "We talked about this. I thought the rent money was to pay off bills?"

"It is. I promise you, I didn't spend a penny on supper."

She smiled. "I'll go and round up Kasey and Robbie." There was a knock on the back door as she started toward the hall. "Would you get that, honey?"

"Mom…" Lilly started to go after her when the knock sounded again. "Okay, you win," she murmured as she went to the door and opened it. Standing on the porch was their new tenant. He looked as if he'd showered and shaved and he was holding three pizza boxes. "Mr. Cooper?"

"It's Coop." He nodded toward the boxes. "I hope you're all hungry."

What was going on? "Why?"

"I told your mother I was treating tonight. Since you let me move in early."

He took a step toward her and she immediately moved out of his way. "You didn't need to do that. I was going to fix supper."

He put the pizzas on the counter. He placed his hands on his hips, causing his navy T-shirt to stretch across his broad chest and flat stomach.

"If you're making salad, I can help you." He went behind the island counter. "Tell me where the bowl is and a knife."

He already had the head of lettuce under the water washing it. *Well, make yourself at home,* she thought. With no choice but to keep up she retrieved the ingredients.

Within a few minutes they'd thrown together a salad and he placed the bowl on the table when she heard the kids on the stairs. They soon appeared in the kitchen.

"Hey, I know you," Robbie said. "What are you doing here?"

"Robbie," she warned her son. "Mr. Cooper brought us supper."

"How do you feel about pepperoni pizza?"

Robbie's eyes brightened like it was Christmas morning. "It's my favorite."

"I don't like pepperoni," Kasey said. Her thirteen-year-old daughter didn't like much of anything these past months, especially her mother.

"Then it's a good thing that I also brought a vegetarian one, too."

"That's my favorite," Lilly said.

"I'm not hungry." Her daughter pouted.

"You're going to stop being rude and eat." She turned her daughter toward Coop and brushed back her long blond hair from her pretty face. "Coop this is my daughter, Kasey. Kasey, this is Mr. Cooper. He's the new tenant and he was nice enough to bring supper."

"It's nice to meet you, Kasey."

She nodded, but there was suspicion in her large eyes. "Thank you for the pizza."

Lily released a long breath as her mother appeared in the room. "Okay, maybe we should sit down and eat."

Beth showed Coop to a chair at the round table. Once in their seats, Lilly said, "Kasey, I believe it's your turn to ask for the blessing."

She glared at her mother. "Why? I don't have anything to be thankful for."

Lilly felt her cheeks flame in embarrassment. "Okay. Robbie why don't you do it?"

"Sure." He folded his hands and bowed his head. "I'm thankful that I got to go swimming today and now I get pizza, too."

Lilly bit back a groan as she looked at her mother.

"You'll survive, honey," Beth said. "I survived you."

Lilly took charge and said the blessing herself. Once she finished she was grateful everyone concentrated on the food. She wasn't surprised to see her daughter didn't have a problem eating. Finally the kids were excused to go watch television. She wanted to leave, too, but then she'd be just as rude as her kids. She wouldn't be setting a good example and her mother was still there.

Lilly went to the coffeemaker. "Would you like a cup?" she asked Noah Cooper and her mother.

He looked up at her and smiled. "Thank you, I wouldn't mind one."

After her mother declined, Lilly came back to the table, handed him a cup and sat back down. The conversation turned to the repairs of the house.

"You have a wonderful house here," Coop told her mother.

"Thank you. I've lived here since I was a girl. After my parents died, I inherited this house and my husband, Charles, and I raised Lilly here. I want it to go to her." She looked sad. "But I can't keep up with the repairs."

Coop reclined in the ladder back chair. "From what I can see the structure is in good shape. Most of the damage seems to be from the elements. The porch needs some of the boards replaced. The concrete steps are crumbling. That should be the first repair."

Her mother looked at him. "I'm not sure I can afford you."

A slow, easy smile spread across Coop's face. "I work pretty cheap. If you buy the materials, my labor is free."

Beth smiled. "I like that, but it doesn't seem fair."

Coop looked thoughtful. "How about if you throw in a few meals?"

Lilly wanted to object. The last thing she wanted was another man around. "Noah, I would think you'd get pretty tired of spending the evening with bickering kids."

"I think I'm up to it," he assured her.

She was losing this battle. The privacy she needed so desperately since her marriage and life fell apart.

She looked at the good-looking man across from her. All she wanted was a nice quiet summer break. But it didn't look like that was going to happen now.

CHAPTER THREE

LILLY tried to ignore him, but how could she ignore a shirt-less man right in her line of sight? And that was exactly where Noah Cooper was. It was only eight o'clock the following morning, and the man stood on a ladder scraping the peeling paint off the back of the house.

Finally giving in to the old adage "What was the harm in looking." And that was exactly what she did. Look.

She leaned a little to the side of the kitchen sink to get a better view. To see how his faded jeans fit across his nice rear end. How those muscles over his back and shoulders bunched with his movement. The tiny beads of sweat that gathered along his spine and ran down into the back of his Levi's.

She blew out a breath. Whoa, must be the heat getting to her. She turned away. She didn't need to get all worked up just noticing a man, especially not a man who'd just arrived in town.

One thing for sure, she didn't need any more compli-cations in her life, or in her kids' lives. After the disaster with Michael, she couldn't risk it.

The man she thought she loved and respected had seemed to change overnight. Something she couldn't be-lieve at all. She'd known Michael Robert Perry since grade school. They'd gotten together in high school and then went to the same college. There had never been anyone else.

She thought she knew the man she'd married at twenty. Until he turned into a stranger and he started keeping secrets and then finally left her and the kids. It was still hard to believe that man she'd loved and shared two children with had abandoned his family.

Worse, after the divorce, he refused to even see his own children. Gave her full custody. He did pay child support for a while, but she soon discovered that he'd mortgaged their house for the business. She couldn't afford the payments.

Thank God she could come back home to live with her mother. Her kids needed the stability of having their grandmother there when she couldn't be. And they helped each other out financially.

Even after all that, Lilly kept praying that the old Mike would return and want his family back. But he never showed up, never spent time with Kasey and Robbie.

For the past two years, she had to deal with the aftermath of two kids losing a parent, then the finality of his death a few months ago. Robbie seemed to be doing fine, but not Kasey. She'd always been Daddy's little girl. Now, she was sad and angry.

Lilly could still remember when the sheriff came to tell her about Mike's death. He said it was suicide.

That day part of her died, too. For the man who'd been such a big part of her life. The man who she'd vowed to love, honor and cherish. Mike's desertion from his family had ended that long before his death.

"What happened, Mike?" she breathed, unable to stop wondering if she'd been the cause. "Why did you change? What made you stop loving us?"

Lilly glanced out the window again to see Coop. Why

was she drawn to him? Okay, it had been a long time since she'd had a man's attention. And Noah Cooper was easy to look at, in a rugged male sort of way. He wasn't afraid to get down and dirty. She felt heat rush through her as he climbed off the ladder. He went to the hose, turned it on and raised the spray over his head, allowing the water to run over him.

"Oh, my," she groaned as the water dripped over his chest and ran down to his waist. He reached for a towel and she couldn't look away from the erotic scene as he rubbed the towel over his muscular chest and arms. Already the sun had bronzed his skin, contrasting with the white line along his waistline.

He turned and exposed his wide back and she caught a dark mark on his left shoulder. A tattoo. She squinted but couldn't make it out.

"What's so interesting?"

Lilly jumped as her mother came into the kitchen. "Nothing, just Mr. Cooper working on the house."

Beth glanced out the window and grinned. "And what a nice view, too." She sighed. "Oh, to be young again."

Lilly tried to concentrate on her coffee. "Mother, at your age."

"At any age," she countered. "There's nothing wrong with enjoying looking at a man, Lilly. You're a healthy, young woman."

"And I'm a mother and a school principal. I have to set a good example."

"Then show your kids that you haven't shriveled up and died. Get out there and live."

Before she could put up any argument, the back door opened and Mr. Sexy walked in. He'd put on his shirt, but it wasn't buttoned yet.

He nodded. "Mornin', ladies."

Her mother smiled. "Good morning, Coop. I see that you've already started working."

"Wanted to get an early start before the heat really hit," he informed her as he went to the coffeepot and poured some into the mug.

"Then you're in time for some breakfast. Lilly is about to fix hers." She turned to her daughter. "You wouldn't mind cooking up some eggs for Coop? With Jenny out with the baby, I promised to help out at the Blind Stitch this morning."

Lilly didn't like this. "Sure." She went to the stove, grabbed the skillet, then went to the refrigerator to take out the bacon and eggs. "How do you like your eggs, Mr. Cooper?"

"Any way is fine."

Lilly cracked the eggs into a bowl. "Scrambled."

"Well, I better get going," her mother said. "I'll be home for lunch. Anything you need from the store?"

"No, Mom, I can't think of anything."

"Okay, bye." She was out the door and Lilly was left alone with the first man who, in a long time, made her aware of the fact she was a woman. She didn't need this right now.

Coop watched as Lilly Perry stomped around the kitchen. He knew she wasn't happy about him being here, but he had no choice. He had a job to do.

"Here, let me help." He went to the stove and took the bacon from her and began to lay strips in the flat skillet.

"You don't need to do this. You and my mother have a deal."

He looked at her, catching her pretty blue eyes. "That's right, your mother and I made a deal. You had nothing to do with it." He felt a stirring and glanced down at the sizzling bacon. "This is your vacation, Lilly."

"I have children, Mr. Cooper. I don't get a vacation, summer or otherwise."

"Okay, then I don't want to add to your chores."

"Cooking breakfast isn't going to kill me."

He stopped her. "What's the problem? No one can help you?"

She stiffened. "It's easier to go it on my own."

"Sounds like you've been let down a lot."

They both held the standoff until the bacon began crackling. He turned down the flame.

"You've made it clear you don't want me here," he told her. "And I'm not sure why."

"I don't know much about you. And with you being around my kids and mother…I need to watch out for them."

"I'm only here to do a job, Lilly. I swear I'm not going to hurt you or the kids." Not physically anyway. But she'd already been hurt by the man she loved. "Do you really think Alex Casali would hire me to work for him, if he wasn't sure that I'm reputable?"

Lilly glanced away and concentrated on cooking the eggs. "The past few years haven't been very good ones for my kids. Their dad left them, and he never even came to visit." She looked up at him again. "I don't want Robbie to get attached to someone who'll be leaving, too."

"That's understandable, but you can't stop your son from making friends with people. That isn't healthy, either."

She turned off the stove and took two plates out of the cupboard, then split the eggs between them. He placed the bacon on the paper towel as she made toast. Once the job was complete, she carried the plates as he grabbed two filled coffee mugs, then followed her to the table.

She sat down across from him, but she refused to look at him. He knew Lilly would be a tough sell.

"Would you rather I move out of the cottage?"

Her fork stopped halfway toward her mouth. "Would you?"

"If you can't trust me around your mother and kids. Yes." He was taking a big chance here. "I'll leave, Lilly. The last thing I want is for you to think of me as a con man…or worse. I've done nothing to cause you to think like that. So maybe the solution is to just leave and move into the motel out on the highway."

He took a bite of his eggs then found it was difficult to swallow. He realized that he didn't want Lilly to think the worst of him. But her husband had made sure that she had a hard time trusting.

"I can't ask you to do that. It's my mother's choice to rent to you." She put down her fork. "You're right, Mr. Cooper, you haven't done anything to cause my rude behavior. Please accept my apology."

"I'll accept it under one condition."

She waited.

"You better start calling me Coop, or I'll have to call you Principal Perry."

She fought a smile and lost. "Okay, Coop. What brought you to Kerry Springs?"

"Plain and simple, a job."

He watched as Lilly began to eat and that helped him relax a little. "I'm from El Paso, Texas. Born and raised there."

"Any family?"

He shook his head. "Not much. My mother took off years ago. My father left long before that, before my birth. I had a half brother, but he was killed a few years back. He left a wife and a baby daughter behind." They were the reason why he wanted Delgado. And he was going to get the bastard. "I keep in touch with them."

She looked concerned. "I'm sorry. How did your brother die?"

"He was a police officer shot in the line of duty."

He pushed his plate away and began to stand. "I should get back to work."

Lilly reached across the table and touched his arm, causing him to pause. The warmth and softness caused a reaction. His throat grew dry and his gut knotted in need. Something he hadn't felt in a long time.

"Is there anything I can do to help you?"

A dozen different pictures shot through his mind. He never thought of a school principal being sexy, but that was until he ran into Lilly Perry.

"I wouldn't mind if you'd keep some iced tea handy."

"That's all I can do for you?"

She didn't want to know what he wanted her to do for him. She'd throw him off the property.

"That's all for now."

Two hours later, Coop moved his work area to the shaded porch. It wasn't much cooler, but at least the sun wasn't frying his back.

"Hey, what are you doing?"

Coop glanced down to see Robbie behind him. "I'm trying to get your grandmother's house ready to paint."

"Oh," the boy said. "Did she say you can do it?"

"Yes, and she's happy about it."

The kid kicked the floor with the toe of his shoe. "Can I help?"

Coop got off the stepladder. "Well, that depends on how hard you want to work. I don't like quitters."

"I'm not a quitter."

"Good, 'cause I pay a good wage and I want the best workers."

Those big eyes widened. "You're gonna pay me?"

"Sure." He looked around. "I could use someone to sweep up all the paint chips."

"I can do that," he announced.

"Okay, you'll need a broom and dustpan. And I have a trash can at the side of the house."

Robbie took off, calling out, "Be right back."

Smiling, Coop went back to work, but was quickly distracted when a work truck pulling a trailer stopped at the curb. The vehicle had the lettering Perry's Landscaping on the side door.

Coop felt the rush of adrenaline. "Okay, it's time to do my real job," he murmured and climbed off the ladder.

Two Hispanic men got out of the truck and took the mower from the back of the trailer. It looked like they were here for the yard service. Then he spotted the driver as he climbed out.

Also Hispanic, he was above average height with a slender build and thick coal-black hair. He might have been dressed in a work uniform, but Coop doubted he was a day laborer.

He took a closer look at the man. Since he'd studied Delgado's actions for a few years, he recognized this man's familiar features. And this guy could be his twin.

And it looked like he was going to get the opportunity to speak with him as the worker walked to the porch.

"Hey, man, are you painting the house?"

"You could say that."

"Good." He studied Coop for a second or two. "Rey Santos."

Coop didn't offer his hand. "Noah Cooper."

"Where's your crew?"

"You're lookin' at it."

Santos frowned. "You need men? I can get you some workers. At a good price, too."

He bet he could. "No, thanks, I work solo."

The two studied each other when Robbie came back with the broom and pan. He stopped on seeing Santos.

"This guy here is all the help I need," Coop said.

Santos nodded. "Is Mrs. Perry around?"

"No!" Robbie said. "She had to leave."

Coop could see the boy's fear. Why? Had Santos been bothering the family?

"I'll catch her later."

Robbie waited until the guy left the porch, then went to Coop. "What is he doing here?"

"Doesn't he work for the lawn service?" He knelt down in front of the boy. "Is something wrong, Robbie? Did that man do something to you?"

The boy shook his head. "No, he yelled at my mom once. She told him to go away. And a long time ago he worked with my dad. He got mad when I was there with my dad."

Coop hated to pump the boy for information, but he didn't have a choice. "Is it a secret?"

"Kinda. I promised my dad I wouldn't tell anyone."

"Tell anyone what?"

Robbie was silent, but fear showed on his face. "It's okay, Robbie." He needed to know if Santos had threatened him. "You can't get into trouble now."

"One day I was supposed to stay with Kasey, but she got mad at me and made me stay in my room. I sneaked out and went to see my dad at work."

Bingo.

The kid looked frightened. "Don't tell my mom. She'll be sad again."

Coop gripped the boy's shoulders. "We don't want to

make her sad. Just tell me one thing. Did Santos see you with your dad?"

Robbie shook his head rapidly. "No, Dad made me hide when the man came in his office. They were yelling and I got scared. After that man left, my dad said it wasn't a good idea for me to come back. Then he…died."

The boy's tears tore at Coop. "I know it's hard to lose someone you love. I lost my brother."

The boy's lip trembled. "Did you cry?"

Coop didn't even hesitate. "Yeah, I cried a lot. He was my only family."

"My sister says boys aren't supposed to cry."

"She's wrong. Everyone cries when they're sad. It helps to heal your heart. And you know what else helps?"

The boy wiped his nose with the back of his hand and Coop gave him his bandanna to use. "No, what?"

"To remember good things about that person."

The kid looked thoughtful. "You mean like how much my dad liked peanuts. He used to hide a jar, but he'd share with me."

Coop's chest tightened. Mike Perry sounded like a decent guy. So what the hell happened?

"That's a good one," he said. "I remember that my brother used to get into my baseball cards. I yelled at him because he used to get them dirty and bend them. A few years ago for my birthday, Devin found me a rookie Nolan Ryan baseball card."

The boy grinned. "Dad liked him, too."

"Well, maybe…we can go to a game sometime." Coop stood, knowing this conversation was getting far too personal. "Right now, we better get to work."

Lilly walked down the hall to close the front door to block out the noise from the mower, and keep Santos away. That was when she heard her son's and Coop's voices.

She hadn't planned to eavesdrop, but she couldn't stop when Robbie started talking about his father. Since her ex-husband's death, both children had clammed up and refused to say anything. So to discover that Robbie had gone to see Mike was a shock. She also learned what she'd suspected—that Mike had been involved with Santos. She didn't want to think about that. Mike was gone, and she and the kids had to deal with the aftermath.

Lilly's focus turned back to the man who seemed to be getting through to her son. She liked how Coop handled the situation by telling his own stories. She'd known from their breakfast conversation that Noah's brother had died. Maybe that was what he and her son had in common.

She felt her chest tighten. She wasn't the only one who had lost. She might have misjudged Noah Cooper. Over the past couple of years, she had a lot of anger to deal with and she'd been lousy at it. She hated the fact that the entire town knew her business. Thanks to Mike, aspects of their divorce were made public. Yet that didn't make it right to take it out on every man who came into her life.

She pushed open the screen door and stepped out on the porch.

"Hi, Mom," Robbie called. "I'm working for Coop. And guess what, he's paying me, too." He returned to sweeping paint chips as if proving he could do the job.

"That's good, son. Since you're working so hard, why don't you go and get you and your boss some bottles of water?"

"Okay." He dropped the broom and ran into the house as Lilly turned to Coop.

"Thank you for working with Robbie. He hasn't had much chance to be with many men."

"It's easy. He's a great kid. I take it that he didn't have much time with his father."

She didn't want to go into it, so she just shook her head. "I'm sorry, I don't mean to pry."

"It's true. Robbie and Kasey hadn't had much time with their father the past few years." She swallowed hard. "I made it nearly impossible."

Coop took a step toward her, but she raised a hand. "I was too demanding after he'd left us. I made all kinds of rules and stipulations about his visitation. Finally Mike stopped showing up at all."

She heard Coop curse. "Did the custody agreement give him a fair amount of time with the kids?"

She nodded unable to speak.

"Well, then, if he loved his kids, he would have found a way."

Suddenly they weren't alone. Rey Santos walked out from beside the house. She shivered as the man smiled at her.

He turned in her direction and came up the steps. "Mrs. Perry. I would like to speak with you."

"I'm afraid I don't have the time right now."

"This will only take a moment. Stephanie wants to know if you have gathered up the rest of Mike's things."

Lilly's sigh was audible. "Tell my sister-in-law that there is nothing left of Mike's in this house. I left anything that was his behind."

Rey Santos didn't look happy as he took a step closer. "If you are keeping any paperwork about the business, Stephanie has the right to them."

Lilly felt Coop's presence. She hated the fact that she liked having him close. "I suggest you tell Stephanie to talk to the sheriff. He took all I had in for evidence." She made that up.

"I will relay the message," Santos said.

"And tell her I no longer need the lawn service," Lilly said. "The cost is too high."

Something flashed in the man's deep-set eyes. It was almost threatening. "*Si, signora,* I'll relay the message to her."

He spoke in Spanish to his crew and they climbed into the truck and drove off.

Lilly released a breath as her body sagged against Coop's. For a second she let herself feel safe and cared for. And a whole lot of things she shouldn't be feeling. Reality quickly returned and she moved away.

"Want to talk about it?" Coop asked.

Lilly shook her head. She couldn't let this man get in. To make her feel again. "Anything you want to know is public record. Ask anyone in town."

His dark gaze met hers. "Maybe I only want to hear your side of the story."

"I wish I had one, but it's still all a mystery to me."

CHAPTER FOUR

LATER that afternoon, Lilly tried to control her anger, but then her worry took over.

"Where are you, Kasey Elizabeth Perry?" She punched in her daughter's cell phone number again. It went straight to voice mail. She left another message. "Kasey, it's Mom, you better call me."

She tossed the phone on the kitchen counter as Robbie came in the back door.

"Hey, Mom, look." He held up a five dollar bill. "Coop paid me for helping him. He said I did a good job."

"That's great, son." She forgot her worry for a moment and hugged him. "I'm so proud of you."

He pulled back. "And I'm going to work tomorrow, too."

Was her son bothering Noah? "Are you sure Mr. Cooper needs you tomorrow?"

Robbie bobbed his head up and down. "Yeah, Mom, he said he needs me to help mix the cement. So I hafta be at work at eight sharp. I'm going to put this in my bank."

Her son shot down the hall and Lilly started to call him back to go help look for Kasey when there was a knock on the kitchen door.

Noah Cooper stuck his head in. "Could I speak to you a minute?"

"Of course. Is there a problem? Is Robbie too much? You don't have be his babysitter."

He smiled at her. "No! No, the boy's been great. A hard worker, too. I just wanted to check with you to make sure it's okay for him to help tomorrow. I won't let him get overheated, or go over more than a few hours."

She didn't want this man to be so considerate. It would be safer if she could stay indifferent, but he was slowly winning her over. "I'm surprised Robbie has stayed interested this long. But since he's so eager, I don't have a problem with tomorrow."

He frowned at her. "Is something wrong?"

Her first reaction was to deny it, but she found herself saying, "My daughter isn't home yet, and she's not answering her cell phone."

He stepped into the kitchen. "Do you know where she went?"

"Supposedly with her friend, Jody. I called her mother, and no one's home." Lilly sighed in frustration. "I'd be really angry if I wasn't so worried."

Noah walked to her, looking so big, strong and reassuring. "It's going to be okay, Lilly. We'll find her."

She knew she shouldn't take his help, but it felt good not to have to do this on her own for a change. She'd deal with the regrets later.

For the next thirty minutes, they looked for Kasey. Coop had loaded Lilly and Robbie in his truck, drove around the neighborhood, then stopped at Kasey friend's house. No one was home. Next came the park and a pizza place. Still no sign of the girl.

"Mom, is Kasey in trouble?" Robbie asked from the backseat.

"Yes. She didn't call me to say she was going to be late."

"Is she gonna be on *'striction?*"

Coop could hear a mother's fear in Lilly's voice. "It's restriction, and that's between Kasey and me. Right now, I just want to find her."

They parked on Main Street and checked the ice cream parlor. The kid behind the counter told Lilly that both girls had been in, about an hour ago.

After thanking him, they walked outside. "What about the quilt shop?" Coop suggested. "Would she go to see her grandmother?"

"I didn't want to worry her." Lilly frowned. "But I guess we better go tell her. Maybe Kasey told her something, since my daughter doesn't talk to me these days."

Coop knew the girl had an attitude. Didn't most teenagers? Of course, a lot had happened in the girl's life lately.

He opened the door to the Blind Stitch and allowed Lilly and Robbie to go in ahead of him. The shop had a few customers milling around, but Beth walked over immediately to greet them.

"Hi, Robbie." She hugged her grandson and smiled at her daughter. "I didn't expect to see you here."

"We can't find Kasey," Robbie blurted out. "She's in trouble, too."

Beth looked from Coop to her daughter. "She hasn't called you, either?"

"No, Mom, she hasn't."

"She stopped by here because her friend had to go home. I told her she could help me here, but Kasey didn't want to. She left about thirty minutes ago. I'm sorry, I should have called you to let you know she was headed home."

"No, Mom. Kasey is thirteen, she's old enough to take responsibility."

"I'll keep looking," Coop said. "Give me your cell number," he told Lilly. After putting it in his phone, he added,

"I'll check the video arcade across the street. Is that one of her hangouts?"

Lilly shook her head. "Absolutely not. We've tried to close the place down because there have been rumors of drug activity there. But my daughter has been doing a lot of things I never thought she'd do."

She looked up at him with those baby blue eyes. "I've got to find her, Noah."

He gripped her hand. "We will, Lilly. You stay here, I'll be back." He'd searched for many kids over his years in law enforcement, some cases turned out good and some bad. He prayed this would be a good reunion.

He headed out the door and jaywalked across the street to the Dark Moon.

It definitely wasn't a family friendly place. Dim and dingy, with black walls and eighties strobe lights. The crowd was older. Teenagers and adults seemed to be wasting away the day, pouring money into machines. Maybe wanting more, like drugs.

He walked around the numerous video machines, the rhythmic sounds and the flashing lights stimulated his senses as he searched the arcade's customers. He was about to give up the search when he spotted a blonde girl. She was dressed in a short skirt and a fitted T-shirt, revealing far too much.

He tensed, seeing her companions, two teenage boys who looked to be about sixteen and very interested in the pretty blonde. One kid had his hand on her arm. This wasn't good.

He walked to the group. "Kasey Perry," he called over the noise. "What a surprise to find you here."

The girl's smile disappeared as he approached them. "Huh, Mr. Cooper," Kasey said. "What are you doing here?"

He looked at the two high-school-aged boys. They had lanky builds, but were nearly as tall as he was. "Oh, I don't know." He gave them a warning look. "I thought I'd soak up some of the local atmosphere. Are these boys friends of yours?"

Coop got a little pleasure watching the kids frown at his description.

"Yeah, Randy and Jake, this is Mr. Cooper. He rents the cottage from my grandmother."

Coop reached out his hand. "Nice to meet you both. So you're both just hangin' out for the summer?"

"We're waiting for football camp," Jake said. "We're gonna play varsity this year."

"Heh, that's cool," Coop told them, folding his arms across his chest. "I was a quarterback in high school. We went to state." He glanced around the arcade. "If you find you're getting bored they could use some strong backs at AC Construction. If you can swing a hammer, look me up there, Noah Cooper. Everyone calls me Coop."

Their eyes lit up. "Uh, thanks." The boys wandered off, seeming to decide hanging around wasn't leading anywhere.

Coop turned back to the girl. "I think you better call your mother." He handed her his phone. "Now."

She didn't move. "What if I don't want to?"

"You know, Kasey, I took you for a smart girl, but I think I'm mistaken. I get that you're angry, but acting like this isn't helping. If you wanted to punish your mom, okay, you won. She's been worried about you. Now, call her."

"I'll get grounded."

"No kidding. Even if you don't call you'll get that. You did this, not her."

"She's too strict. I can't go anywhere."

"You have to earn trust for that," he explained. "And

doing something like this stunt shows poor judgment and immaturity."

She gave him a defiant look. "This isn't your business."

"Okay, let me tell you some hard, cold facts. Those older boys you think are so cute, they wanted to do more than play video games with you. You could have been in big trouble. And it's my business because your mother needed my help today."

He nodded to the phone. "Now, it's time to take your medicine and call her."

It was after ten by the time Lilly got the kids settled for the night. She'd tried to calmly talk with Kasey, telling her the importance of staying in touch by phone. The scary thing was her child wasn't listening to a word she said. In the end, Lilly had grounded her daughter for a week, no phone or computer.

In reality, who was being punished? Exhausted, she walked out on the side porch with her glass of wine. She sat down on the railing and took a sip, hoping the alcohol would soothe away all her fears, the feelings of inadequacy and loneliness.

It had only been a few months since Mike's death, but the past two years had been hell. That was how long she'd carried the guilt about failing as a wife. Now, she was failing as a mother, too.

She heard a door shut and looked around to see Noah coming out of the cottage. He walked along the lighted path toward the porch. She didn't want to talk to anyone, but she knew she owed him more than just a brief thank-you for today.

With a bottle of beer in hand, he stopped at the steps. "Would you mind some company?"

Okay, so the man was considerate. "Sure."

He came up the steps, wearing a clean pair of jeans and a dark T-shirt. His cowboy boots made a tapping sound against the wood floor. She caught a whiff of his soap as he walked by her.

He leaned against the post. "Did your daughter survive your wrath?"

"Barely. Remember, I'm a trained professional. A school principal knows the right buttons to push. According to my daughter, I committed a crime taking away her social life, her phone and computer."

In the shadows, she could see his nod. "With me, I hated when my mom wouldn't let me leave the house. But now everything is done through texting, or the internet."

He looked at her for what seemed like an eternity. "How are you doing, Lilly? It had to be rough not knowing where your daughter might be."

There he went, being nice again.

"No, it wasn't easy and I owe you a big thanks. And it's not bound to get any easier for a long time. Mike was the one who could deal with Kasey's moods. Now she blames me for him being gone."

"She has to blame someone. You're the closest and the one she feels most safe with."

Lilly looked at him. The night's darkness was an intimate setting. "Were you a psychologist in a previous life?" She took a sip of wine. She didn't need it; this man could quickly go to her head—if she let him.

"No, I just made my mother's life difficult too many times to remember."

"For how long?" she asked hopefully.

"Too long. She's gone now." He sighed. "I wish I'd been a better son."

She was curious. "What about your father?"

"He wasn't in the picture." He shrugged. "So I don't remember him much."

"So with your brother gone, you're all alone."

Coop didn't want her to see that much of himself. "I have a sister-in-law and a niece. I should stay in touch more." Just not when he was working undercover.

"You should. But you shouldn't have to subject yourself to listening to a woman crying in her wine."

"No one is forcing me to do anything. And I doubt you complain much, Lilly." He took a drink of his beer. Mainly because he was fighting the urge not to get too personal. "I wish I could tell you that everything will turn out all right, but I can't. You've got good kids, just hang in there."

The moonlight illuminated the area as she looked at him with those big eyes. Man, she was stirring feelings in him, and that was dangerous for both of them. He needed to redirect his thoughts, to business. "Do you get any help from their aunt?"

"Stephanie? She's been trouble from the get-go. She's a lot younger than Mike. He even helped raise her. Then he trained her in the family business after their parents passed away."

"So she has the business now," he coaxed for more information.

Lilly turned and looked at him. "It might be a coincidence, but a lot of the trouble between Mike and me started when she got more involved with the company."

Go easy, he told himself. "Didn't your husband run things then?"

"He did the books, but the day-to-day scheduling of the work crews was Stephanie's job. And for a while they were doing great, the money was rolling in. The only problem was Mike was working more and more hours as the business expanded. Then Rey Santos came in as a manager for the crews. And I thought that would free Mike up and he could cut back on his hours. But Stephanie and Rey started dating." She shivered. "Nothing changed. Then our marriage started…falling apart and finally Mike moved out."

She shrugged, staring out at the night sky. "Then one day I got served with divorce papers."

He saw her blink rapidly, her voice grew soft and shaky as she said, "I just never thought he would divorce the kids, too, and then the suicide." She looked at him. "Can you see why Kasey acts up?"

Coop had a dozen questions he wanted to ask her but was afraid to tip his hand. Was Mike Perry a total jerk, or was he the Feds' informant trying to protect his family?

The next day, Coop worked the morning repairing the walkway with Robbie. By noon, he'd sent the boy off to go swimming with his friends, while he went to see about his new boss.

He pulled his truck into the construction site at the west end of town. There were to be twenty-five affordable, two-story homes to be built in the development called Vista Verde. The first dozen homes were to be completed by September.

In fact, Alex Casali was listing the prices well below market value. It seemed the millionaire rancher wanted to pay back his good fortune to the community. The people who qualified to buy a house were low to moderate income families. And there was already a waiting list for the energy efficient homes that included a small park and community pool.

Coop knocked on the construction trailer door.

"Come in," a man called.

He pushed open the door and walked inside. Although the space was large, it still seemed crowded with two men and a pretty auburn-haired woman and two toddlers running around.

The man behind the desk was Alex Casali, a big man with brown hair and gray eyes. He was a formidable man until he looked at his wife. Their affection for each other was obvious.

Alex finally noticed him. "Coop. Good to see you."

"Hello, Alex. I thought I'd stop by to see about my starting time, but I can see you're busy. Hello, Mrs. Casali." He removed his hat. "Good to see you again."

"Please, call me Allison. It's nice to see you again, Coop. You don't have to leave, I'm taking Will and Rose home for their nap. I think their dad's had enough of family at the work place." She kissed her husband. "See you later at home." She paused. "By the way, Coop, we're having a barbecue this weekend at the ranch. It's for all the workers on the Vista Verde project. You are invited, and please relay the message to Lilly, Beth and the kids. It's really a community event."

He nodded. "Thank you, I'll tell them."

Alex walked his wife and children out, then returned with a smile. Coop found he envied the man, not for all his money, more so for his life and family. He'd felt the same way around his brother and his wife, Clara. Then he recalled the reason he was here: Devin's death.

Alex walked to the desk. "Sorry the kids like to come and see me at work."

"No apologies necessary. You're the boss."

"Boy, have you got that wrong." He grinned. "My wife and kids run things. And I wouldn't have it any other way."

Casali sobered as the two other workers grabbed their hard hats and headed out of the trailer. Once they were alone, he said, "You ready to start Monday?"

"All set."

Casali smiled. "I hear you've been doing some repairs on Beth Staley's house, too. She's been bragging about you at the shop."

Small town grapevine. "I'm not busy right now, and it's a win-win situation. I get free meals out of it."

"I'm glad you're helping out. That family has had a rough few years. Come on, I'll show you around." Casali picked up a hard hat, handed him one and they walked outside.

They headed along the row of framed structures, the sound of hammering and power saws made it difficult to talk.

Casali walked him to an open field area away from the workmen. "I'll introduce you to my foreman, Charlie Reed. He'll be the one you report to, and he hands out the job schedule." They continued to walk along the recently paved road and they reached four nearly completed homes at the end of the block.

"We're proud of this project and I want the community involved in it as much as possible." Alex studied him a moment. "Sheriff Bradshaw asked me to hire you. I take it there's a good reason for that." He raised a hand. "I'm not asking what it is, I've already got that lecture from Brad." Sheriff Oliver "Brad" Bradshaw was Coop's contact in town.

Casali went on to say, "I only worry about keeping my family and friends safe."

"I don't see why they wouldn't be."

"Well, I'm going to make sure of that. Just so you know, I'll have extra security at the party and on the job site."

"That's always a good idea. It's not unusual to have some vandalism on construction sites."

Casali was a powerful presence. He didn't doubt the

man could take care of himself, or get things done. "Damn. I don't like what's going on."

Coop knew he hadn't fooled this man. He needed to change the subject. He told Alex about Kasey Perry's adventure at the Dark Moon Arcade. "From what I could gather it's not a good place for kids."

"Not even close," Alex agreed. "We've been trying to shut it down the past few years. I even offered to buy it, but the owner refused my offer." Again Alex studied him. "It seems you've gotten involved in a few things since your arrival."

He shrugged. "Just a little painting, and helped Lilly find Kasey. Like you said, it's small-town living."

"As a friend of Lilly and her family, we appreciate it. Maybe it's time I alert the sheriff so he can keep a watch on the place."

There were so many things that Coop didn't feel safe involving a civilian in. If it was Perry who contacted the Feds, that might have been what caused his death. Did he leave behind some incriminating information? Stephanie and Santos were too interested in Mike Perry's things. How far would they go to get it? His main job was to keep Lilly and her kids safe.

That was his number one priority.

CHAPTER FIVE

Two mornings later, Lilly's heart swelled at hearing laughter from outside the window. Her son was again working with Coop. Today, their resident handyman and his trusty helper were putting flagstone pavers over the already patched walkway leading up to the porch.

Coop had convinced her mother it would be cheaper to lay stone over the patched concrete than tear it out and pour a new walk.

At breakfast, Robbie had explained that the big tree in the front yard shaded the sidewalk in the morning so it was cooler to work there. They'd go back to painting when the sun moved from the side of the house.

Whatever Noah Cooper was doing, she wanted him to continue because her son was a lot happier these days. So was she. Her smile quickly died. If only she could say the same for her daughter.

She rolled her eyes at the ceiling, feeling the vibration, hearing the loud music coming from Kasey's bedroom. It was the only thing she hadn't taken away from the teenager.

She knew this wasn't the end to this struggle between mother and daughter. Somehow, Lilly had to figure out a way to get through to her. What terrified her was that she might not be able to.

"Mom! Mom!" Robbie cried and she hurried outside afraid he'd gotten hurt.

A quick scan told her he was fine. So was the man standing next to him, shirtless. She felt a catch in her breath as she eyed that beautiful sculptured chest, flat stomach and…

"Come see." Robbie interrupted her thoughts as he waved her down to the sidewalk.

She descended the steps. "What's wrong?"

"See, Mom. I put my initials in the cement," he told her proudly.

"Yes, you did." She looked down at the "RP" along with the date in the grout beside the flagstone. "That looks great. So does the walk."

"Coop said in a hundred years people will know that we did this work."

She stole a glance at the man who rocked her son's world these days. "That's a lot of hot Texas summers and hard winters."

Robbie nodded. "Coop said you should always do the best job so your work will last. So people can depend on you."

She felt emotions welling in her throat. "That's true. You should be proud of everything you do."

"Do you think Daddy would be proud of me?"

She had to swallow hard as she glanced at the stoic look on Coop's face. "I know he would." She put on a big smile as she hugged her son.

After a moment, Coop spoke, "Hey, Robbie, we need to clean up before we go and get ice cream."

"Ice cream?"

Coop gave Robbie a questioning look. "You did ask, didn't you?"

Robbie looked down. "I guess I forgot. Mom, can we go get some ice cream?"

"How about we eat some lunch, then go."

Robbie opened his mouth to argue, then looked at Coop. "Sure."

Lilly turned to Coop. "It's tomato soup and grilled cheese."

"My favorite," he told her.

"It's my favorite, too," her son chimed in.

Coop picked up his shirt and slipped it on. He hadn't missed Lilly's interest, nor did he mind it, but this was work. He needed to concentrate on doing his job and she wasn't making it easy.

He followed them into the kitchen and heard the music from upstairs. He fought a grin. "I take it Kasey's letting you know she's not happy."

Lilly went around the island and pulled out the flat griddle. "Drama for Kasey started when she was about a year old and it hasn't let up yet."

Coop went to the sink and turned on the water to wash his hands. He liked being in this kitchen. It was a little worn, but he bet there'd been plenty of good times here.

He glanced over his shoulder just as Lilly went to get something from the refrigerator. When she bent slightly, her shorts pulled tight over her shapely rear end and long legs.

Oh, boy. He felt the stirring low in his gut.

As if she sensed his attention, she turned around. Her expression was one of surprise, though there was awareness in her eyes, but she quickly glanced away. "What kind of cheese do you want on your sandwich?"

He shut off the water and grabbed a towel, wiped his hands as he leaned against the counter. "Anything is fine." He'd be damned if he would apologize for staring at a beautiful woman. Wasn't that what guys did? Except he was a Texas Ranger who was supposed to be doing his job, and Lilly Perry was a part of it.

She looked at him again. "Why don't you go sit down? I can handle lunch."

He started to argue when Robbie came running into the room. "Coop! Coop! See what I got." He was holding up a baseball in a plastic case as he climbed up on a stool at the island.

"What do we have here?"

"It's a baseball. See it's got Nolan Ryan's name on it. Just like your baseball card."

"Robbie," his mother cautioned. "Remember that's not a toy. It's valuable."

"I won't take it out," he promised her. "I only wanted to show it to Coop." The boy turned back to him. "He played for the Texas Rangers baseball team. Dad said Nolan Ryan's the greatest pitcher ever."

"I know." Coop took the plastic case and examined the ball to see Ryan's signature. "He had seven no hitters. He was the strikeout king. He was nicknamed The Ryan Express."

The boy's eyes rounded. "Wow! You know a lot."

"That's because I love baseball, too. I used to play in high school." It had been the only thing that kept him out of trouble. "Do you play?"

The boy hung his head and murmured, "I don't know how to catch very good." He looked at his mother. "I don't have anyone to practice with me."

Coop felt for the kid, knowing sports had kept him and his brother off the streets. "I bet you can play tee-ball and learn."

Lilly turned the sandwiches on the grill, surprised at her son's comment. She would have loved to sign him up.

Give him an activity to keep him busy. "If you want to play, I can talk to one of the fathers, maybe they will help you."

"Ah, Mom. I don't want to do that."

Lilly was at a loss. She wasn't much of an athlete, so she couldn't help.

"Maybe I can help you," Coop said. "You got a mitt and another baseball?"

"Sure. I'll go get 'em."

Lilly called him back before he left the room. "First, we eat. So go and wash up and get your sister."

The boy looked disappointed, but did what he was told.

Lilly went to stir the soup, then pulled down the bowls.

"Is there something wrong?" Noah asked.

She hated to say anything critical about his act of kindness. She looked at him. "I'm just a little worried. Robbie has been so excited these last few days with you around."

"So you want me to stop being friends with your son."

She sighed. "No, but he's a little boy who misses his father. Doesn't that make you uncomfortable?"

Coop was more uncomfortable about not being truthful with her. "Look, if you don't want me to spend time with your son, that's your right. Since I was a kid who didn't have a father around, I know it's nice to have another man provide some attention."

"Did you have someone?"

Don't get too personal, he told himself. "My brother and I spent a lot of time at the boys' club." He smiled. "A gruff, old guy named Gus. He told us to leave the attitude at the door if we wanted to come in. He kept all the kids in line."

She smiled, then quickly sobered. "Don't get me wrong, Noah. I'm happy you spend time with Robbie, but I don't want him hurt when you leave."

He went to her. "You mean like their father hurt all of you?"

He saw her hesitate, but also the pain in her eyes. She finally nodded.

"You can't keep your kids from getting hurt, Lilly. They have to get out there and learn to survive, not to be afraid. And they need to learn that from you."

"But Robbie isn't even six."

"And he and his sister have already been hurt. You couldn't protect them from the pain of losing their father." He paused. "You're an adult, and you couldn't even protect yourself."

An hour later, Lilly had to get away from the house. She ended up leaving Kasey brooding in her room, and drove Robbie to the library for the children's reading hour, postponing the trip to the ice cream store. Okay, she needed time to brood after Noah's declaration.

She walked into the Blind Stitch, needing some adult time. Some girl time. As usual the popular shop was busy. Since Jenny was on maternity leave, it had been ever harder to keep up with customers. The regular employee, Millie Roberts, was behind the counter.

Lilly found her mother in the other room of the shop, where they held the quilting classes. Beth Staley was instructing a patron on a quilt pattern. She looked up and smiled, then excused herself and walked over.

"This is a surprise. What brings you in?"

"I miss my mother," Lilly said.

Beth smiled back at her. "That's nice to know. I take it the kids are getting to you."

She groaned. "I know I'm a terrible mother, but I can't wait until the school year starts." And she wouldn't be daydreaming about a shirtless man in her backyard. "So can you go on a break?"

"Of course, if you wouldn't mind going with the QC ladies?"

Lilly knew her mother's good friends of the Quilter's Corner. They meet here at the shop a few times a week. She glanced toward the corner table and waved. "Sure."

Liz was the first to greet her, then came Louisa Merrick, both friends were her mother's age. Caitlin and Lisa were younger mothers, close to Lilly's age. They took up quilting because they could find the time with small children.

"Enjoying your summer?" Louisa asked.

"I have a thirteen-year-old who's bored. What do you think?"

They all groaned in unison, and Louisa said, "I know it's seems like hell, but hang in there. They'll turn out nice like you did."

Lilly arched an eyebrow. "Was I that bad?"

"We all were," Liz announced. "It's all those raging hormones."

"Please, my Kasey is too young to be thinking about sex."

"None of us are too young, or too old, to think about sex," Louisa, who looked lovely and healthy these days, added. Even with the stroke she'd suffered last year there were no lingering effects now.

Liz nudged her. "That's because you got yourself a good-looking husband. And he takes you to all those romantic places."

Louisa turned to Lilly. "It seems Lilly only has to look out her back door to find a good-looking man."

All eyes turned to her and she felt the heat rise to her face. "Mr. Cooper is our tenant. It's hard not to look at him. I mean he's helping with the house."

Caitlin jumped in. "I'd say. I drove by yesterday and saw your sexy tenant on a ladder painting the house. He didn't have his shirt on, and I nearly wrecked my car."

"Maybe I should go for a little drive myself," Liz said. "Is Coop working today?"

Lilly couldn't help join in the laughter. She needed this, more than thinking about a man she had no business thinking about.

After lunch, Coop had returned to work, then the heat got to him and he went in the cottage. He still remembered the look she'd given him earlier. He'd had no right to speak to her that way.

So he'd decided that he'd better make himself scarce and disappear. So why not take the afternoon off?

Well, there were a couple of reasons. He wasn't good at relaxing. He liked to stay busy, and he needed to figure out what was going on with Delgado.

Word on the street said he was relocating his drug business since El Paso was getting too hot. The Feds just hadn't figured out where until they received a message from the informant. Now they were thinking Kerry Springs was at the top of the list. Okay, it was farther from the border, but who'd suspect the picturesque small town would harbor drug dealers?

Now he just needed to find the place. Perry's Landscaping Company? It would be a perfect hideout. Nothing would give him more pleasure than to ship Delgado off to prison for drug trafficking and for the murder of Officer Devin Morales. Plus his possible connection with Mike Perry's demise.

He only had to gather the proof. Where to look: the landscaping business or maybe the video arcade? Delgado wasn't the type who sold drugs on street corners. His known MO was to have gangs distributing the merchandise. Kerry Springs might not have gangs, but every town had drug users.

Coop was getting antsy. He needed to end this and soon. Get Delgado. And the sooner he could make sure that Lilly Perry and her kids were safe, he could leave and forget about her. Undercover work didn't allow for return visits.

There was a soft knock on the door and he closed his notebook and placed it under a toss pillow. He went to answer it and found Lilly standing on the stoop.

She looked pretty in her blue blouse that matched the color of her eyes and asked, "Could I speak with you?"

"Sure." He stepped back, allowing her inside the small area. "Is there something wrong?"

"Yes. I neglected to apologize for my behavior earlier. You're right, Noah, I am overprotective of my children." She sighed. "It's just that when all this happened with Mike, his death was so public, I didn't know how else to handle it except to wrap my kids up and hold them tight."

He shook his head. "I owe you an apology, too. I had no business telling you how to handle your children. I'm a single guy. I don't know anything about parenting." He inhaled her soft scent and nearly forgot his speech. "If you'd like, I'll keep my distance. Don't worry, I'll be the bad guy and tell Robbie."

"Oh, no, Noah. Please, you're the best thing that's happened to my son in a long time. He's been living in a house with only women for the past two years. Now that he's nearly six I see the changes in him." She looked sad. "He's not my baby anymore. And I'm not really sure on how to handle the next stage of his life."

She turned those bright eyes on him and he felt a kick. "All the baseball and Boy Scouts…"

Ah, hell, she was killing him. "I'm sure there are

coaches and Scout leaders who will take him under their wing."

She nodded. "I know, but today was the first time he looked interested in doing anything. So if your offer is still open, I'd be happy if you helped Robbie learn to catch." She held up a hand. "I mean, I know how busy you are with the repairs... Oh, God, how can I ask you?"

"You didn't ask, I offered to help. Lilly, it's not rocket science, it's tossing a baseball with a boy. Besides, I don't start my construction job until next week."

She raised her chin and smiled at him. Good Lord, she was pretty. Her skin was rosy and flawless.

"I have another favor to ask."

She was getting to him. Bad. "Sure."

"Would you please go with us to get some ice cream?"

He smiled. "Okay."

Lilly knew she was acting schoolgirl crazy, and she knew better. Something about this man brought out those silly, giddy feelings in her.

"Thank you. Of course, it's my treat for all the work you've done."

"Sure. I don't have a problem with a lady buying my favors."

"I probably couldn't get much with two scoops of Rocky Road on a sugar cone."

He stared down at her and her heart began to race. "Change that to Cherry Pecan and your smile, and it's worth a lot more."

Oh, boy, she was in trouble. "We better go round up the kids." She scurried ahead of him to the kitchen door and hollered for Robbie and Kasey. Surprisingly they both appeared and followed her outside.

Her daughter headed for the car. "No, Kasey, we're walking."

"Mom," she whined. "It's too hot."

"It's getting rather pleasant," Lilly insisted. "Besides, we're only four blocks from town. I'm a school principal who pushes physical fitness. How would it look if we go driving around everywhere?"

Kasey stomped over to her. "Then I don't want to go."

"You don't want any of Shaffer's ice cream?" She slung her arm over her daughter's shoulder, and she didn't shrug away.

The girl shook her head.

"Well, you still have to go along anyway."

The teenager opened her mouth to complain again when Coop appeared. "Is he going, too?"

"Yep. Looks like you're stuck with me." He motioned to Robbie. "C'mon, Rob. Let's see if the ladies can keep up with us."

The boy looked over his shoulder. "Yeah, see if you can keep up."

Lilly looked at her daughter. "Are you going to let them win?"

Her beautiful child got an ugly look on her face. "I don't care."

Lilly started moving, but kept well back behind the guys. "Look, Kasey, I get you're angry with me. But when you don't obey the rules, there are consequences."

"I know. You run things like a prison around here. I have no freedom."

"I don't think I did at thirteen, either. But you are still young and you went to a place that was off-limits. It's my job as a mother to protect you."

"Fine. I get it, but I don't have to like it." She marched up ahead, past the guys. Robbie took off after his sister and Coop dropped back with Lilly.

"I take it she's still angry with you."

She nodded. "My mother says it's payback for how I treated her."

"You're doing the right thing. Stay on her because it's tough out there."

Lilly frowned. "Is there something you're not telling me? Something more that happened at the arcade?"

He shook his head. "It's just the element that hangs out there isn't the best."

Coop glanced around the tree-lined street, and the manicured lawns and hedges. It seemed like the perfect place to live and raise a family, but looks could be deceiving. "At that age they think they can conquer the world, that nothing can harm them."

"I remember those days. Yet, this town doesn't have the problems that large cities do. We all know each other and watch out for each other."

An older woman standing on her porch called Lilly's name and waved.

"Hello, Miss Olivia. How are you feeling today?"

The fragile looking, gray-haired woman came down the steps as Lilly went to her. They exchanged a hug and he could see her hands were crippled with arthritis.

"I've heard your mother's working at the quilt shop these days."

"She's filling in for Jenny."

A big smile appeared. "Oh, yes, she had her baby, didn't she?"

She nodded. "Sean Michael will be christened next Sunday at church. I bet you can get a look at him then."

"I'll make sure my sister takes me." Miss Olivia patted her hand.

"How is Miss Emily these days?"

A loud sigh. "Sister complains a lot, but she's well. I'll mention that you asked about her." Her expression changed. "I never got the chance to tell you how sorry I am for your loss. Michael was always a kind person to me."

Coop could see that Lilly was uncomfortable. "Thank you," she said and took her hand away.

That's when Miss Olivia took an interest in him. "And who is this young man?"

"Noah Cooper, ma'am." He shook her hand. "I'm a carpenter on the Casali housing project. I'm renting Beth Staley's cottage."

"Isn't that nice." She glanced between the two. "A pleasure to meet you, Noah."

"Well, we should be going," Lilly said, pointing to the kids already nearly a block away. "I promised Robbie and Kasey ice cream."

"Then ya'll run along," she told them.

Coop didn't need to be asked twice as he followed Lilly. "I take it she's been your neighbor a long time."

"Before I was born. She never married and argues with her sister all the time. She's only a few years older than Mom, but has to rely on her sister to get around." She gave him a sideways glance. "But she can dial a phone pretty well, and with the information you gave her, you'll be the talk of the town by tomorrow."

Going inside Shaffer's Ice Cream Parlor was like stepping back in time to the 1950s. The *Happy Days* TV show, Western style.

Robbie and Kasey were already sitting on high stools at the counter, going over the selections on the wall. If ever Coop felt out of his element, this place would do it. His hangout had been a pool hall.

This would be the childhood every kid wanted, and

those who were lucky enough to get it didn't even have a clue how wonderful their lives were.

From a street kid's perspective, one who had to beg, borrow or steal to survive, he knew he'd have been chased out of a place like this. As a teenager, he'd hung out in a pool hall to hustle players, or just helped clean up the place for money.

Coop sat down beside Kasey. She tensed and glared at him.

He ignored it as the teenage waiter appeared. "Hello, Mrs. Perry."

"Hello, Tim. Good to see you're working this summer."

"Saving for a car."

"Are you that ancient?"

The boy's ears reddened. "I was sixteen last month."

"Now, I'm feeling old."

He turned his attention to his other customers, namely Kasey. "What are you going to have?"

"Vanilla," Kasey told him.

Coop frowned. "Vanilla? That seems rather dull from someone so…" He looked at the girl's scrubbed face, a hint of freckles across her pert nose. Those big blue-green eyes. She was the image of her mother. "So daring. So vibrant."

Although Kasey tried to hide it, the compliment affected her. "Sometimes I get Peach or Raspberry sherbet."

He nodded. "I'd go for the Raspberry sherbet."

"I want Chocolate Chip," Robbie said to the waiter.

"And I'll have Mint Chocolate Chip," Lilly announced.

"What about you, Coop?" Robbie asked.

"Cherry Pecan."

While they were waiting as the boy scooped up the cones, the bell chimed over the door. Coop glanced toward the entrance to see a dark-haired woman walk in. He immediately recognized Stephanie Perry from the case files.

In her mid-twenties, she had a husky voice and dressed in a pair of jeans about a size too small, emphasizing her wide hips. She might have been attractive, but her heavy layer of makeup made her look hard.

He tensed as the woman made her way to the counter. "Lilly, I need to talk to you."

Lilly swung around and frowned. "Suddenly you want to talk. No, we have nothing to say, Stephanie."

"There's a lot to say. You have some of Mike's things and I want them back."

Lilly didn't want to air any dirty laundry in front of the kids or the rest of the town. She stood and walked across the store and her ex-sister-in-law followed. "I don't like you attacking me, especially in front of my children."

Stephanie folded her arms over her breasts. "Then give me Mike's things."

"And for the hundredth time, I don't have anything of his. When he moved out, he took almost everything. When I moved out, I only took my things, Mike came by and took the rest. What exactly are you looking for?"

Mike's sister glanced away. "Papers from the business. They must have been in his home office."

"I left Mike's home office alone. So I don't know what happened to his papers after that."

Stephanie glared. "You're lying. You never liked me so you're getting back at me because Mike divorced you."

Lilly was thrown off guard. Not that Stephanie's words hurt anymore, she'd said worse during the years of her marriage to her brother. "I'm not going to listen to this again. I want you to stay away from me and the kids. Go and run your business."

Stephanie glared. "You'll be sorry if you're keeping anything from me."

"Is there a problem?"

Lilly felt Coop come up behind her. Even though she could handle her sister-in-law, she liked having him there.

"Not anymore. I think we've finally settled it. Haven't we, Steph?"

Lilly got a little satisfaction at using the nickname that her sister-in-law hated.

Stephanie looked at Coop. "Got a new boyfriend so soon, Lilly? How long before you drive him off?"

Coop did something that surprised her. He slipped an arm around her waist. "Oh, I don't think this pretty woman could drive me away with a shotgun." He smiled. "In fact, you'll be seeing me next week. I'm one of Casali's carpenters on the housing project. So get used to it, Ms. Perry, I'm going to be around a long time."

CHAPTER SIX

LATE the next evening, Cooper sat on the sofa in the cottage. He had to figure out a way to stop thinking about Lilly Perry in any way but as a lead for his job.

He knew he had to play the part and get close to the family. It was getting harder all the time, especially when he'd put his hands on her narrow waist, or been close enough to breathe in her soft scent.

He cursed and stood. It was time to get to work.

He waited until dark and dressed in a black T-shirt and jeans and running shoes. He left the cottage, bypassing his truck, and headed out on foot down the alley to avoid being seen by the family. People had to think he'd been home all night, plus he didn't want his vehicle parked outside where he was doing surveillance.

He took alleyways as much as possible until he got to the edge of town. Perry's Landscaping and nursery had ten acres that had a tree and plant business, in addition to the professional lawn service. There were several buildings and a half dozen work trucks parked in a line all enclosed by a chain-link fence.

He checked the area for any sign of electronics or otherwise. There wasn't a security guard or a dog, so he found a weak spot in the fence and climbed through. Staying in the shadows, he made his way past the greenhouse and a row of buildings, including one that was labeled as the office. There was a light on inside.

He made his way around to the back and to an open window. That was where he heard the voices.

One was Stephanie Perry and the other was a man with a thick Spanish accent. Santos aka Delgado.

"Rey, you can't bring another shipment in here," she said. "Not yet."

"You worry too much," Santos said.

"We still haven't found Mike's papers."

"I curse *su hermano* for all our troubles. He could have had so much if he'd gone along with us. I'm thinking he lied about the papers."

"What if he didn't? You can't bring in the shipment."

"I can't stop it. It's crossed the border, so it's not safe to leave it out there unprotected. And my men need their supplies to fill the demand."

Coop wondered if it had come through Ciudad Juarez at El Paso, or Nuevo Laredo at Laredo.

"And what about Lilly?"

Santos cursed in very colorful Spanish. Coop recognized several unflattering words directed at the woman.

"You've got to get inside the house," he told her.

"How can I do that?" Stephanie argued. "She warned me off. She's the type that'll call the sheriff on me."

"Then you'll wait until everyone leaves, or maybe I can persuade her."

"Good luck with that," she said.

A shiver snaked down Coop's spine. They would go after Lilly? No way in hell. He stole a look into the office as Santos whispered something in Spanish. Stephanie giggled, then Rey grabbed her roughly. "My luck is always good."

Then his mouth ground over hers. She let out a groan

of pain and fought him to break free. "Hey, that hurts," she cried, trying to push him away.

"That's it," he growled. "Fight me."

Santos forced Stephanie down on the desk, and Coop moved out of sight, leaving the lovebirds. He figured he wasn't going to get any more information tonight.

Coop made his way off the property and headed back to the house. He needed to make some calls, to figure out his next move. One thing there was no doubt about: drugs were coming into Kerry Springs. His job was to stop them.

The next morning, Lilly was up at dawn. She was never one for sleeping in. Having been a teacher most of her adult life, she found early mornings had helped keep her sanity. And she'd always been the one to get the kids up and moving, allowing Mike to sleep in. He did so without a problem. Of course, he'd worked ten-to-twelve-hour days. Had that been to stay away from her? She shook away the thought. *Don't go there. It's too late for regrets.*

She made her way down to the kitchen. She had dressed in shorts and a sleeveless top, ready for the hot day that had been promised.

She glanced out the window toward the cottage, surprised to find the door open. She was even more surprised when Noah stepped out into the small covered porch.

"Oh, boy," she breathed as he leaned against the post, dressed only in a pair of jeans. Her gaze lowered to the top two buttons that were undone, causing his pants to ride low on his hips.

For heaven's sake, she'd seen a man shirtless before. Oh, but never had she seen anyone who looked like Noah Cooper. His muscular chest and broad shoulders looked like they could carry the weight of the world. She lowered her eyes to his flat stomach. That was an understatement.

He had what they called a six-pack. The man had to work out all the time.

Slowly his gaze went to the house and the kitchen window. Busted. Their eyes met and she was frozen in place. It seemed like an eternity that his eyes held her in a trance, then finally he raised his mug toward her like a salute, turned and walked back inside the cottage.

Lilly released a breath and sank against the counter. What was she doing? She wasn't the type to ogle a man. In school she'd been the shy, studious one. Mike had been her first boyfriend, then her husband.

"Morning, dear," Beth Staley said.

Lilly jumped as her mother strolled into the room. "Oh, hi, Mom."

Beth frowned. "Is something wrong?"

A lot. "No. You just surprised me. What are you doing up so early?" She glanced at the clock. Six-ten. "You don't have to go to work until nine."

The older woman smiled and went to pour some coffee. "Oh, I don't know. I guess I couldn't sleep."

Lilly examined her mother closely. Something was different about her. "Did you get your hair cut?"

"Yesterday. Do you like it?"

The shorter cut would be easier for her to care for. "I like it. The color is pretty, too."

"It's just a shine Cassie talked me into trying. It's to take the yellow out of my gray."

Her mother had great hair, thick and healthy. Lilly looked over the fifty-eight-year-old widow. At five foot four, she was trim and kept in shape. She had pretty green eyes and a warm smile.

There were other subtle changes about her. Her style of clothing was different today. She had on white capris and an aqua-colored knit top, partly covered with a multicolored blouse.

"Mom, you look…so pretty."

She sighed. "Thank you."

"Is there some reason you're all dressed up this morning?"

She gave a sheepish grin. "Could be."

Lilly folded her arms and waited. "Well, aren't you going to tell me?"

Her mother actually blushed. "I have a breakfast date."

"A date?" She swallowed. "You mean a date, date?" Her mother hadn't dated since her dad's death ten years ago. "Who?"

"Close your mouth, daughter. It isn't becoming."

"Mother."

"Okay, I'm meeting Sean Rafferty for breakfast."

The good-looking, charming Sean Rafferty? "What? How long has this been going on?"

Beth sent her daughter a sharp look. "That's not anybody's business, but we've spent some time together. We happened to run into each other in San Antonio last month when I was shopping there.

"Sean asked me to lunch, and we found we enjoyed each other's company. And since we're both so busy this is the only time we have to see each other."

"You're right. It isn't my business. I just thought Millie Roberts had a thing for Sean."

Her mother sighed. "I know, but Sean doesn't feel the same about her. We find we have so much in common, and there is that spark. Oh, plenty of sparks."

Lilly wanted to put her hands over her ears. Was this more than a platonic friendship? *My mother is in a love triangle.*

"And I need to tell her, today," Beth said.

"Yes, you should," Lilly agreed. "She'd be hurt if she heard it from someone else." What else could happen this morning? She'd ogled a man, and her mother was dating. Suddenly the music vibration started upstairs in Kasey's bedroom.

This was going to be an interesting summer.

It was after seven o'clock before Coop was off the phone with his captain relaying details about Delgado and the possible drug shipment coming to Kerry Springs. That was enough information to have more men posted around the landscaping business, looking for any unusual activity.

They wanted to get Delgado this time. In the past he'd managed to slip through the cracks, and no one would rat him out. Mike Perry might have tried, but he was dead now. They needed to find the proof that Mike had planned to give them, and before it got into the wrong hands.

He stood and looked out the window. He wasn't sure he should go to the house for breakfast. He couldn't deny the attraction between himself and Lilly. It would be easy to let things happen, but in the end he would have to leave when the job was done. Except Lilly Perry would be hard to say goodbye to.

There was a soft knock on the door. He opened it to find Robbie. "Hey, Rob, you ready to work?"

He nodded. "Mom said to tell you breakfast is ready."

Coop hesitated, but seeing the bright look on the boy's face, he nodded. "Good, I'm starved."

The boy didn't move. "Coop, can I ask you something?"

They walked along the path together. "Sure."

"If you're not too busy later, can you play catch with me?"

"Sure. We could probably find some time."

"Oh, boy. Thanks."

Robbie ran ahead and through the back door. Coop smiled and followed him inside where he found a brooding Kasey at the table and her mother at the stove making pancakes.

"Hi," he said to Lilly as he went behind the island. "Need some help?"

"Sure. You can set the table. Plates are up there."

He reached overhead and brought down four plates. He grabbed flatware and headed to the table. "Here, Kasey, make yourself useful."

The teenager was about to argue, but Coop gave her a look that had her changing her mind. He went back to get the orange juice and glasses. In a few minutes they were all seated at the table and enjoying a nice breakfast.

"Where's Beth?"

"She has an…early appointment."

Robbie chimed in, "She's having breakfast with Mr. Rafferty."

"Robbie, where'd you hear that?"

"You and Grandma were talking."

"How many times have I told you that eavesdropping isn't polite."

"I don't know what that means."

"I mean, you shouldn't listen to other people talking."

"But didn't she go with Mr. Rafferty?"

"Yes, but Grandma's business isn't to leave this house. If she wants other people to know she'll tell them."

He took a bite of pancakes and after swallowing, he said, "Kinda like when Daddy left us, and people started sayin' bad stuff?"

"And we don't want that to happen again."

The silence was deafening and Coop could see Lilly was uncomfortable.

"Hey, Rob, why don't you go grab your ball and glove and we'll toss a few?"

"Oh, boy. Can I, Mom?"

"Finish your milk, then you're excused."

He grabbed a few more bites of food, then drank up and ran off. So did his sister, although she didn't ask permission.

The room was quiet with only the sound of footsteps overhead. "It was rough for you and the kids, wasn't it?"

She nodded. "Even though there were a lot who stood by me, there were many who speculated on what happened between Mike and me. I was a bad wife. Had he met someone else? It all happened so fast. As if overnight my husband had changed and I couldn't stop it." She toyed with her coffee mug. "I guess I didn't protect my children as well as I'd hoped, because in the end, their father abandoned them, and I can't forgive him for that."

If nothing else, Coop hoped he could learn the truth for her, but first he had to find it. Then they would both have answers to all the questions.

"I'm sorry, Lilly."

She turned those hazel green eyes toward him. "Why? None of this is your fault. Mike was an adult. He made choices. All bad, but he made them." She chewed her lower lip. "Worse, I know it had something to do with Stephanie."

Bingo. "Why? Did your sister-in-law try to break up your marriage?"

She sighed. "You saw her yesterday. She was always jealous. She was the baby of the family, ten years younger than Mike. He spoiled her rotten because their father ignored her. After their parents died, Mike took over the business, and that included helping Stephanie."

Coop carefully worked for information. "It seems that the business is prosperous."

"That's thanks to Mike. He expanded it to do land-scaping and new construction and he opened the nursery on the property. We all sacrificed, too, helping to secure the future. Now they're without a father, and my kids get nothing.

"Why is that? Aren't his children in the will?"

Lilly shook her head. "Mike signed a survivorship clause, leaving everything to his sister. Stephanie walks away with it all, the business that rightfully should go to my children. She and that slimy boyfriend, Rey Santos, get everything."

"Do you suspect something isn't right?"

He watched her anger build along with her tears. "I don't care anymore, Noah. Mike's gone and the kids are without a father. All I want is for Stephanie to stay away from my family. We want to move on with our lives."

Lilly stood. "Excuse me, Noah, I need to get to the store this morning. If you want anything more, help yourself. I'll get Kasey to do the dishes."

He got up, too, and stopped her before she left. "If my opinion means anything, I think you're one hell of a woman, Lilly Perry. A man would be a fool to leave you."

An hour later, Coop was calling himself every name in the book as he stood in the Staley backyard. He had no business saying anything to Lilly at breakfast.

Dammit. The woman was getting to him, and he had to stop it. He had to find a way to stay focused on his job. Not how much he wanted to pull her into his arms, feel her body against his. The problem was he wanted more than just to ease the loneliness; he wanted a connection with another human being.

"Heads up, Coop."

He looked at Robbie to see the ball come flying. He was

using the first baseman's mitt that had once been Mike Perry's. He reached out and managed to snag the errant throw.

"Okay, Rob. Here it comes." He tossed the ball in the air. "Now get under it. That's right, look it into your glove."

The ball dropped in the kid's glove and Robbie let go with a cheer. "I did it. Did you see, Coop? I did it."

"I sure did. You kept your eye on the ball and you weren't afraid." He tugged on the boy's cap. "Good job." They did a high-five.

Just then Lilly's compact car turned into the driveway and parked at the garage. Robbie went rushing toward her. "Mom, I caught the ball."

She got out of the car and hugged her son. Something inside Coop's chest tightened at the sight. His mother had never been affectionate with him or Devin. She was too busy for them most of the time.

Robbie pulled her by the hand. "Come on, Mom, we'll show you."

"Okay."

The boy told her where to stand, then rushed off to about fifteen feet away. "Throw it to me, Coop."

Coop nodded. With a glance toward Lilly he turned back to Robbie. "Okay, keep your eye on the ball like the last time." He lofted the ball in the air, praying that the boy could get it.

"*Look* it into your glove," he coaxed until he heard the familiar thud.

He'd never seen a brighter smile than the one on Robbie's face. Then he turned to Lilly. He was mistaken. She was beaming.

"Oh, Robbie, I'm so proud of you," she cheered.

The boy ran to his mom. "Wow. I'm getting better. I'm gonna go tell Kasey." He took off running.

Coop didn't move, but Lilly did as she came up to him and touched his arm. "Oh, Noah, how can I ever thank you? I haven't seen Robbie this happy in a long time."

He could feel the warmth of her hand. "I just tossed him a ball." He resisted squeezing her slender hand, but he refused to let her go, either.

"You spent time with him. He hasn't had any male attention in a long time."

"Yeah, a boy needs that."

She finally took her hand away. "I bet you helped your brother a lot, too."

"I tried. Our mom was gone a lot."

She nodded. "I know that feeling. That's why my mother is a godsend. Speaking of which, she's invited Sean Rafferty to dinner tonight."

"Not a problem. I can go to the diner downtown."

"Noah," she said with a smile. "You're invited to come, too. It's just a heads-up, they are officially dating."

Coop smiled, finding he liked being included. "I hope he's worthy of her."

"Sean Rafferty is a very nice man. And according to the ladies my mother's age, quite a catch. It seems Beth Staley has done something about a dozen women in town haven't been able to do—caught Sean Rafferty's eye."

"So would you like me to grill him on his intentions?"

She laughed at that. He liked the sound and the way her hair brushed her cheek. He had to resist not to reach out and touch her. Damn, he was getting in deeper and deeper.

CHAPTER SEVEN

LILLY watched as the sensible Beth Staley seemed to become more and more flustered as she prepared supper for Sean Rafferty. All she could say was the man had better appreciate it.

And the second Sean walked into the house carrying a bottle of wine from his son's vineyard and roses from his garden, sending a special look to her mother, she felt her own heart do a tumble.

"Sean," Beth breathed.

"Hello, lass," he returned with that dreamy Irish brogue and an engaging smile. He leaned down and kissed her cheek.

Then he looked up and saw her. "Hello, Lilly. It's good to see you again." He held out the wine. "Here's a little contribution to the dinner."

"Nice to see you, too, Sean. And thank you. This chardonnay will go well with the chicken."

He tossed her a wink. "It's nice to have access to a winery."

Lilly smiled. The new label Rafferty Legacy graced the golden bottle. "This is lovely, thank you. How's the family?"

"Wonderful. Sean Michael is a blessing, and a strapping lad he is. Much like his da and his uncle."

"He's adorable," Beth added. "Jenny brought little Mick into the shop this morning."

"Sorry I missed that." Lilly was disappointed. "Will they be coming to the Casali's barbecue?"

"Of course," Sean said. "Jenny says she's had enough of staying home. She can't wait until she gets back to the shop."

Lilly felt out of touch. "Jenny's coming back to work?"

"Part-time," her mother told her. "She's going to set up a nursery in the back, and also use the upstairs apartment for naps and feedings."

Lilly would have loved to stay home with her babies, but she didn't have that choice. She'd had to go back to teaching to help support the family.

Suddenly there was a noise from above as her kids made their way down the stairs. Robbie was the first to speak. "Hi, Mr. R."

"Hi, Robbie. I hear you've been practicing playing baseball."

Her son beamed. "Yeah, Coop's helpin' me. I catch pretty good now."

Sean turned to Kasey and grinned. "Well, who's this pretty lassie?"

Lilly held her breath waiting for her daughter's reaction. She actually smiled. "Hello, Mr. Rafferty."

He reached for her hand. "You look like your mother and grandmother. Beautiful."

"Oh, Sean." Beth blushed. "She doesn't want to hear that."

"Why not?" He looked at the three generations of women. "You ladies are a picture."

Lilly smiled. "Thank you. I'll go check on supper." She took off, not wanting her mother to leave her guest.

Lilly walked into the kitchen as Noah came in the back door. "Sorry, I'm late. What can I do to help?"

He was dressed in a nice pair of jeans and a collared shirt. Handsome as usual.

"Not much to do," she told him, trying to ignore her racing heart. "I'll just put the food in the bowls and carry it out to the dining room." She stopped and sank against the counter. "I can't believe it. I mean I believe it because my mother is an attractive woman, but I just never thought she'd seriously date someone."

Seeing Lilly's anxiety, Coop went around the island to her. "It's a good thing, isn't it? I mean this man makes her happy, doesn't he?"

She nodded. "That's just it. What if she wants a life of her own, and the kids and I are in the way?"

Coop frowned. The Beth Staley he'd gotten to know in the past week would never turn away from her family. "I doubt that. She loves having you here."

"But it's different now. She's dating. She's never dated, not that I know of."

"Look, your mother has just started seeing this Sean. It might not lead to anything."

She pointed to the other room. "You didn't see how the two of them were looking at each other." She paused. "I don't want her to feel she can't think of her future because of us."

Coop reached out and gripped her upper arms. She was a combination of softness and strength and he found he liked both. "Lilly, you can't do this to yourself. Your mother seems like a person who speaks out when there's something on her mind. If there was a problem with you and the kids being here, I'm sure she'd talk to you about it."

She raised those green eyes to meet his and it sent a jolt through him. "I'm being silly, right?"

Hell, he wasn't sure of anything, except he had to fight to resist her. "No, not at all." He managed to release her and when he tried to step back, she reached for his hand.

"Noah, thank you."

He nodded, feeling the warmth of her hand. "Anytime."

"Lately it seems you spend all your time talking me in from the ledge."

"That's me, rescuing damsels in distress," he said, trying to make light of the situation.

"It's not the usual me. There's been a lot of changes in my *once-organized* life. I actually run an entire elementary school, and do it very well."

He smiled. "So you're a real tough guy underneath."

She began to laugh. "It's a hard job but someone's got to do it."

He couldn't help himself and did the same.

Once she sobered, she reached up and brushed her lips across his cheek. "Thank you again, Noah."

He could only nod and glance away, feeling a burn throughout his body. What was she doing to him? "Hey, we better get this food on the table. I'm hungry."

"Then I better feed you."

Five minutes later, they'd managed to carry the food in and called everyone to the table. Sean was filling the wineglasses as the kids took their seats. Once seated around the linen-covered dinner table, he realized it had been a mistake to sit so close to Lilly.

In the short time Coop had been in the Staley household, he'd been made to feel like a part of this family. Something he'd never felt growing up.

Most of the time it was just him and his brother. His mother either worked, or had a date with some guy. Why would Cindy Cooper-Morales want to hang around a slum apartment with her kids, anyway?

This was the homiest he'd ever gotten, and it was a farce. He had to remember that, too. Not real. Remember why he was here and not get personally involved.

However, the family thing might be a good cover, for people to think that he was dating Lilly. But the last thing he wanted to do was lead her on. She'd been hurt and lied to enough.

In the end, a lot of people could be hurt. This time, he could be included in the scenario.

Saturday was a perfect day for a barbecue, sunny, but not too hot. Coop drove Lilly and the family in his truck. It was silly to take two vehicles since Beth would meet Sean there and he'd take her back home.

Once again, he was geared up to do his job. The problem was he had to use Lilly and the kids for cover. If something didn't happen soon, he had to wonder if his captain would pull him from the operation.

Of course that didn't mean that Santos and Stephanie were going to stop being a threat to Lilly. The entire family could be in danger. He needed to get more information and soon.

Every night this past week, he'd returned to Perry's Landscaping, hoping to learn more, or at least see something happening. Nothing. He hoped today would provide a break, because his captain wasn't going to leave him here forever.

"I can't wait to ride the horses," Robbie called from the backseat.

Lilly smiled. She knew Alex would have horse rides for the children, along with swimming and several games so parents could enjoy themselves.

"What are your plans, Kasey?"

She shrugged. "It's going to be boring." She stared out

the window. "I wanted to stay home but you wouldn't let me."

"Come on, Kasey, it's going to be fun," her grandmother coaxed. "A lot of your friends will be here today."

Lilly agreed. "Yes, they will." She reached back and touched her daughter's leg. She felt her tense. "Just give it a chance, Kasey. If you're going to be so bored this vacation, I could put you into summer classes."

That got a cold stare. "You can't do that."

"I'm not going to put up with your bad attitude for the next two months. Your choice, Kasey, so think about finding something constructive to do. And I'm not talking about you staying up in your room all day, either."

Lilly turned back around and saw a happy look on her daughter's face when they drove through the large, iron gate that read, A Bar A Ranch. They stopped beside the ranch hands standing on either side of the road, greeting each carload of guests and giving directions.

Noah continued on past the ranch compound to the wooded area that was Cherry's Camp.

The summer camp for handicapped kids was opened a few years back by Alex and Allison. Their eldest daughter, Cherry, had been in a wheelchair after a childhood accident. Now she was fully recovered and walking.

The facility wasn't scheduled to open until the following week, so there was plenty of room for today's barbecue.

Once parked, they all got out and walked past several of the family cabins to the large two-story structure where several barbecues and smokers were set up on the deck.

Inside the main hall there was a huge common area with a wonderful stone fireplace. Already friends and neighbors were milling around the area. The building also housed an exercise room, an indoor pool and a large kitchen and dining area.

Along the walls were tables of food; everyone brought a dish to share. By the looks of the limited space left, no one would go hungry.

"Lilly."

She turned to see her friend and new mother coming toward them. In her arms was her new son. "Jenny. I was hoping you would be here."

"Wouldn't miss it."

Lilly smiled down at the baby. "Oh, and look at this guy." The baby was dressed in a little shirt that read, Cowboy In Training along with jeans. "Oh, could I hold him?"

With Jenny's nod, Lilly scooped up the infant in her arms. She inhaled the baby's scent, the warmth of having his sweet weight against her. She rocked him and kissed his head as she smiled and cooed at his sweet face, then looked up and caught Noah watching her.

She glanced at her mom and Jenny. They were talking and not paying attention to her. "I get a little carried away," she finally said to him. "There's something about new babies."

Coop nodded in agreement, but in truth he had never thought much about babies. He had a niece, but with his work, he'd never been around her much. Yet something about Lilly holding the kid got to Coop. He didn't like that, reminding himself he needed to stay focused on his job.

Lilly looked away when her kids were asking her questions, then Kasey and Robbie quickly took off.

Beth was looking around. "Jenny, have you seen Sean?"

"He's in the kitchen, dropping off his barbecue beef and chicken. He'll be out here soon."

"So I'm finally getting to sample some of this famous sauce I've heard about," Coop said.

"You haven't been to Rory's Bar and Grill?"

Coop shook his head.

"Well, you're in for a treat," Beth said. "People come from miles for a taste of his sauce. He's been talking about marketing it." Then she realized how much she was giving away. "Well, he's talked about it a little."

"What a great idea," Lilly said.

It didn't take long before Sean Rafferty came out of the back followed by two younger men. Coop recognized one as Jenny's husband, Evan. Seeing the close resemblance to the other male, he guessed him to be Matt Rafferty. The one who had quite the reputation with the ladies.

Sean grinned when he spotted Beth. "Beth. You made it." He kissed her on the mouth, then hugged her close. "I missed you." He had no trouble showing affection, and he wasn't the only one in the family. His sons followed suit, hugging Beth. So everyone was happy with the couple.

"Hello, Coop." Sean shook his hand. "I'd like you to meet my sons, Evan and Matt. Boys, this is Noah Cooper. He rents Beth's cottage and works for Alex."

"Good to meet you," Coop said to Evan. "I saw you at the hospital, but I guess you were a little preoccupied."

Evan laughed and hugged his wife close. "Yeah, Jenny has a tendency to distract me, along with this little guy."

"Can't say I blame you. Congratulations."

"Thank you."

Coop looked at Matt. "Hello, Matt. I hear you run a vineyard and a cattle ranch."

The younger brother put on a grin. "Among other things. So you're working for Alex?"

"I'm a carpenter."

He nodded. "And a lucky man to be staying with Beth and Ms. Principal here?"

"I'm renting the cottage out back."

Beth jumped in. "Coop is also helping out with some repairs on the house."

Matt nodded, but didn't respond. Was the guy wondering if there was something going on between him and Lilly? Had the two dated before?

There were loud voices and they all looked to see more people coming. "Oh, the Merricks are here," Lilly announced. "Look at Louisa, doesn't she look great? I hear her and Clay are off on another trip soon."

Coop recognized the older gentleman as Senator Clayton Merrick, soon to be retired after he finished this last term. He wasn't sure who the others were.

"I didn't expect to see her here," Matt Rafferty murmured.

Coop turned around to see a petite raven-haired woman. She was beautiful. Seemed Matt Rafferty wasn't exactly happy.

"Of course Alisa would be here," Beth said. "She's the project manager on Vista Verde."

"What's the matter, Matt?" Evan asked as he nudged him. "Wouldn't Alisa give you the time of day?"

"I don't need her to give me anything."

Jenny stepped in. "Oh, come on, Alisa's not like that. You just don't know her." She smiled at her brother-in-law. "It couldn't be anything you said or did to her, could it?"

Matt shrugged, but Coop could see that the woman got under his skin. "Doesn't matter," he said. "There's too many other women around." He wandered off and found two willing females to spend time with.

Beth patted Sean's hand. "He just needs to find that special one."

Sean didn't look convinced and suggested, "Why don't we go and see Clay and Louisa and find out about their latest travels?"

Beth looked at her daughter. "Would you mind?"

"Of course not. Go and enjoy yourselves."

The baby had fallen asleep and Lilly gave him back to Jenny.

"You have the touch," the new mother said. "I better go put him in his carrier." Jenny walked off with her husband.

With everyone's desertion, that left Coop with Lilly. "My mother looks so happy." She beamed. "I couldn't have picked any better guy for her. Sean raised his sons on his own after his wife left them years ago. Never complained, and his boys came first. So he hasn't seriously dated anyone." She sighed. "What am I doing? They only started seeing each other and I have them married. Maybe it's just a friendship."

He cocked an eyebrow at her. He'd seen how Rafferty looked at Beth. He might be in his late fifties, but the man's look showed desire.

Coop started to respond when he saw Stephanie Perry walk in with Santos. "Your sister-in-law has arrived."

"My *ex*-sister-in-law. Darn, I was hoping she wouldn't show today. If she comes anywhere near me, I'm calling the sheriff."

"No need, I'm here," he told her, knowing he wanted to keep an eye on Santos. He only hoped that he'd show his hand today. Maybe get some idea what was going on. They could slip and say something. It was a long shot, but that was what he lived for.

After eating far too much, Lilly ended up alone at the table. Robbie and Kasey had both finished and run off with friends. Since her daughter had been so cheerful, Lilly let her off restriction for a few hours. Her mother was with Sean and their friends. Noah had taken off, to speak with Alex about something work-related.

Okay, pity party of one.

"Well, well, sister dear. Seems you're all alone. Again."

Lilly tensed as she turned to see Stephanie. "Go away, or I'll get someone to remove you." She glanced across the room but no sign of anyone to help. She got up to leave.

Stephanie stopped her. "Just give me a moment."

Lilly sank back down on the bench. "Why should I? All you do is harass me. You have everything already, what else could you want from me?"

Stephanie raised a calming hand. "Just something that's gone missing. Some tax information that Mike had. I just thought he might have left a box that got mixed up with your stuff."

Lilly didn't trust her. "Why would I have anything of Mike's. He's been gone nearly two years."

Stephanie seemed to stumble over her words. "Well, we need all the tax records for the last seven years. We're being audited."

Lilly shook her head. "I don't have it."

The bigger woman was crowding her space. "Maybe there's a box somewhere. In the attic, or a closet."

"I told you it's all gone. Now I've got to go."

"To your new boyfriend?"

Lilly froze. "That's my business. We're done here."

"But you need to help me find the papers."

"For the last time, no. And if you don't stop harassing me, I'll get a restraining order."

The woman looked shocked, but then a sneer came across her face. "You don't have the guts."

* * *

Coop had been keeping a close watch on Santos all afternoon, but the man had stayed pretty close to Stephanie. They spent time with neighbors and friends, also with the hosts Alex and Allison Casali. One thing for sure, Rey Santos seemed to be well acquainted with just about everyone in town. Of course he helped run a business that serviced a lot of the residents of Kerry Springs.

Was this a dead end?

Coop was about to give up on anything happening when a Hispanic man came up to Santos. Their body language told him that this was more than just a friendly conversation. After a few minutes, the stranger walked off. Next Santos glanced around and he, too, started to leave the barbecue area. He acted as if he were going for a smoke, holding an unlit cigarette as he backed into the wooded area behind the cabins.

Keeping his distance, Coop followed Rey through the trees behind the cabin. Santos kept walking, looking over his shoulder.

Coop circled around to the other side, using the trees and brush for cover. If Rey was going for a smoke he was walking quite a ways to do it. He finally stopped in a clearing.

Behind a large tree, Coop waited and soon two more men made their way out of the trees.

He crouched lower and managed to move a little closer so he could try to decipher their voices from the music and noise coming from the party. They were speaking in Spanish. No surprise.

Growing up in El Paso, he knew enough to get by, but with everyone speaking at once, he only managed some key words, like "delivery" but he needed to hear a time or a date.

What the hell was being delivered? Drugs? Was this

what the informant was trying to tell them? *Give us the times and dates of the deliveries.* Was this what Stephanie and Santos wanted from Lilly? Damn, he needed more answers.

Suddenly he heard his name and turned around to see Lilly coming toward him. Coop glanced toward the clearing. The others had heard her, too. The men dispersed, except for Santos who headed their way.

There wasn't anything Coop could do but fake his way out of it. When Lilly finally reached him, he grabbed hold of her and pulled her against him as his mouth covered hers.

CHAPTER EIGHT

LILLY was caught totally off guard when Noah reached for her. He wasn't gentle as his mouth closed over hers, but raw hunger didn't allow finesse. Nor did she want it to.

Slipping her arms around his neck, she had no plans to stop what was happening. The feel of his mouth against hers stole her breath, causing her heart to drum against her ribs. The sound pounded in her ears. Mostly she reveled in the joy of being in Noah's arms.

With a groan, he moved his hands over her back and pulled her tighter against him. She reacted with a moan and opened to him. It didn't take long as his tongue moved against hers, sending shivers down her spine.

Then his mouth broke away, but she didn't have a chance to miss it as he nibbled his way along her jaw to her ear.

"Lilly… We're being watched, follow my lead."

Watched? Who was watching? She managed to nod. Then his mouth returned to hers. She couldn't stop a moan as he worked his magic again.

"Perdon, señora."

Lilly jumped and turned around to find Rey Santos. "Oh, Rey."

The man's somber look slowly turned into a grin. "Sorry to disturb you." He glared at Noah. "I wanted to make sure you are all right."

Lilly worked to control her breathing, but couldn't speak.

"Why wouldn't she be?" Noah asked. "Except maybe from people sneaking up on her," he went on as he pulled her closer.

Santos's eyes narrowed. "Maybe the woods isn't the safest place to be…with your *mujer.*"

Noah's woman. Lilly had to admit she liked that idea.

"We wanted to be alone," Noah told him. "I had no idea the woods would be so crowded."

Santos continued to stare at him. "Next time be more careful." He turned and marched off.

Noah dropped his arms from her and she swung around. "Okay, what's going on?"

Coop refused to put Lilly in any more danger. "I'm not sure. Santos has been acting strange and I followed him out here. He met up with some men. I didn't want him to know I was watching him, and when you came…" He looked at her. A mistake. Her lips were still swollen from his kisses. She was killing him. "Why were you looking for me?"

"Wait! That kiss was to distract Santos?"

He started to nod, but then confessed, "Okay, I might have gone a little overboard, but you're a very tempting woman. I apologize for taking advantage of the situation."

This time she seemed flustered. Hell, didn't she know how appealing she was? And that was something he couldn't let tempt him again. "Why did you want to see me?"

She shook her head. "Stephanie cornered me in the hall. She insisted I look for a box with Mike's tax papers. Then when I told her I didn't know anything about a box, she got irritated again." Her gaze met his. "It's not tax papers is it, Noah?"

He tried to act innocent. "What else could it be?"

"I don't know." Lilly was worried. "The way Mike had been acting the past year…and Stephanie's boyfriend… Could it be something illegal?"

Coop shook his head. "There's no proof."

"I didn't ask that. There's something going on. I know it. Ever since Rey Santos started working in the business it's been different." She tried to swallow her panic. "Oh, God, was Mike involved, too? That has to be it. I know this is Stephanie's fault. I'm going to give her a piece of my mind."

Lilly started to walk off and Coop caught her by the arm. "No, Lilly. If what you suspect is true, it could be dangerous to confront them."

Her gaze met his. "Then what do I do, just let them keep threatening me?"

"Maybe we can find what they're looking for. Do you think that your husband might have left something with you?"

She'd been trying to rack her brain. "I can't swear to it. I know, I told Stephanie I didn't have anything of Mike's. And I didn't take anything from his home office, but that doesn't mean things didn't get mixed up."

Coop was grasping at anything that might trip her memory. "Would he leave anything important behind?"

She hesitated. "All the important documents and papers went into the wall safe at our house."

A wall safe? "Well, whoever lives there now has probably already looked inside."

She shook her head. "The house is empty. Besides, the safe is well hidden. Mike had it put in himself." She sighed. "Maybe I should remind Stephanie about it and she can look for herself. Then she'll leave me alone. No! I should go. There could be other important papers in the safe."

If there was proof of Santos's or Delgado's illegal activity, he didn't want to hand it over to him. He was pretty sure Mike Perry died because of this. These guys weren't taking any prisoners. It wasn't safe for any of them. "I don't think it's safe for you to go into that house. Not alone."

"Then come with me."

Three hours later, Coop didn't want to think about the rules he was about to violate. Lilly was going to break into her old house. Since nothing he said or did had changed her mind, his only choice was to go along as her accomplice.

Once the kids were shipped off to friends' houses for a sleepover, and Beth and Sean left the Casali barbecue for an evening of dancing, it was only the two of them heading back to town.

"Do you still have a key?"

"Yes," she said, digging through her purse. "I haven't been able to take it off my key ring." She glanced across the dark truck cab. "How pathetic is that?"

"Not pathetic at all. It was your home, where you raised your kids. More than likely the bank changed the locks."

"Probably. After Mike's suicide there was an investigation for a few days."

The night sky didn't allow him to see her face, but he could hear the pain in her voice. "Did he die at the house?"

"Yes," she said in a soft voice. "The garage. He died of asphyxiation from carbon monoxide."

Coop knew all this. "God, Lilly I'm sorry."

Lilly nodded, trying to keep it together. "Not many people want to live in a house where someone has died."

"Then you shouldn't go back there, either."

"Yes, I should. I need to end this once and for all. If Mike did something illegal, I need to know. I have to protect my kids. If he didn't and we find these papers, Stephanie will be out of my life for good."

When Coop reached across the truck console and took her hand, it gave Lilly the strength she needed. It was wonderful to get comfort and reassurance, but she felt something else was happening between them. It had been since the kiss. If she was truthful, it had been since the moments he met this man.

"At least you'll know," he said.

They were silent as they reached town. Lilly gave him directions to the house. Since it was after ten the neighborhood was quiet. They didn't take a chance of being noticed and parked in the alley down the street.

With the aid of a penlight, Lilly led him through the gate and the backyard toward the one-story, ranch-style home.

Silently she took out her key and attempted to work the lock. It didn't fit any longer.

"Darn. I guess it was too much to ask to make this simple." She glanced around. "There's only one other way to get inside."

"How's that?"

"The window in the garage doesn't lock. And if they hadn't changed the door to the house, it can be easily shimmied."

She started to go and Coop stopped her. "I can't let you go there. I'll go through the window."

She nodded.

He took off, found the window and with a couple of whacks on the frame, it gave way. After raising it, he climbed inside and across the empty double car garage to the door leading to the house. It wasn't locked. He went inside, and quickly searched for a security alarm. There was none. He then unlocked the back door for Lilly.

Lilly didn't want to look around. She didn't want to remember her time here. The months she and Mike had spent remodeling the kitchen. How the kids had sat at the bar eating breakfast, doing their homework. All the wonderful times in this house. Then it was gone.

She made her feet keep moving down the hall to the den. Mike's office. She opened the door to find it empty, too, but it didn't stop the flash of memories. The big old schoolteacher's desk she'd found and sanded and stained for this area.

No! She wouldn't give in to the memories. That life was over. With the aid of the light, she took Noah to the wall with built-in bookcases that now were empty.

"Where is the safe?"

She handed him the light. "Hold up the light." She reached for the middle shelf and unlatched a hook, then swung it out to reveal a safe built into the wall.

"This would be hard to find." Coop felt hopeful. But were they going to hit the jackpot this time? "Do you know the combination?"

She nodded. "Unless he changed it, it's our birthdays. She began to spin the dial first right, then left, then right again. She paused, then pulled down on the handle. It opened.

Coop shined the light inside the box. Empty. There was nothing. If there ever was anything, it was gone now.

Lilly's shoulders sagged. "Nothing. I'm sorry."

She looked over her shoulder and her hair brushed against his face. He should move away, but didn't as he breathed in her soft scent. "Don't apologize to me," he told her. "I wanted to help you find something to get Stephanie off your back."

He found he wanted to reassure her that everything

would be okay. He couldn't do that until he found the proof that Mike had promised them.

"You're getting pulled into this mess."

"Do you hear me complaining?" Coop asked.

"But if Rey and Stephanie are doing something illegal…" She gasped. "What if they caused Mike to end his life?"

From the conversation he'd heard the other night, Stephanie hadn't sounded too broken up over her brother's death. "You still have no proof."

"Then I'll find some."

He didn't need her guessing about this. "Whoa, Lilly. That could be dangerous."

All at once the silence was disturbed by the sound of breaking glass. Lilly started to speak, but Coop placed his finger on her lips, knowing they had to get out of there.

"Is there another way out?" he whispered as he shut the cabinet door and clicked off the penlight.

Lilly took him across the den to a door that led into a small pantry and the kitchen. They barely got there when they heard voices, then people entering the den.

Coop left the door open a crack and took a quick glance at the intruders. No surprise, it was Stephanie and Santos. Seeing them go straight to the cabinet and wall safe, he knew they were after the same papers. Coop had little doubt that Mike Perry had been their informant.

If he didn't have Lilly with him, he'd have stayed and taken his chances to learn more, but her safety was his first concern. He whispered against her ear, "We need to get out of here. Now."

Twenty minutes later, Coop's heart rate hadn't slowed. Looking across the truck, he saw that Lilly wasn't in much better shape.

He turned down her street and saw Sean's car parked in front of the house. Great. He didn't want anyone else knowing what had been going on tonight. There were too many civilians involved already. He parked in front of the garage.

He climbed out and went around to Lilly's side. "We need to talk."

He walked her toward the cottage and they went inside. After flipping on one table light, and closing the drapes, he took two beers from the refrigerator. He twisted off the caps and handed her one. "Drink."

She did as he asked and he followed suit. He motioned to the sofa. "Sit."

Lilly shook her head and took another drink. "I can't. What is going on, Noah?" She brushed back her hair, revealing the panic on her face. "I don't even know the man I was married to."

"You're not sure Mike was involved in anything illegal."

She gave him an incredulous look. "Then why does Stephanie want these so-called papers so badly? They broke into our house. If they are looking for tax papers, would they go that far?"

Coop shrugged, wishing he could push her suspicions aside. "And we don't know what we're dealing with, either. Not until you find some proof. And I'd say that's too dangerous."

"Then I'll go to the sheriff."

"And tell him what?" He didn't want her involved any further. "We broke the law tonight, Lilly. We trespassed and broke into a bank-owned property."

"So did Stephanie and Rey."

"I know, but nothing was found or taken, and since we're the only eyewitnesses…"

She looked about to cry. "I can't believe any of this. This is a bad dream and I want to wake up."

Coop didn't know what to say. "I'm sorry, Lilly."

"No! Don't you feel sorry for me. My marriage ended a long time ago. It's the children I'm worried about. They've suffered enough. Mike's abandonment. His death. You can see I'm losing Kasey." She brushed a tear away as she paced the small room. "Who knows what's going to happen to Robbie when he gets older? When he really needs a father."

Coop tried to stay uninvolved, but this woman drew him and he had to go to her. "Come on, Lilly. Robbie and Kasey have you. You're their strength. You're a great mom."

She blinked those watery eyes at him. "I'm so tired of being strong. I can't…"

She fought him, but he pulled her against him, and she finally gave in. He held her, hearing her sobs, absorbing her tears in his shirt. It was hard not to react to her sadness.

After a few minutes, Lilly quieted and looked up at him. His gaze went to her mouth as he remembered how she tasted, how she made him feel.

She was feeling it, too. She breathed his name and he was gone. He lowered his head at the same time she rose up to meet him. The instant his mouth closed over hers, nothing else mattered as he got lost in her.

The kiss was deep and searching from the start. He couldn't seem to get close enough, wanting to feel every inch of her, tasting her sweetness. It only made him ache for more.

Not breaking the kiss, he pulled her down onto the sofa. He wanted her body pressed against his.

"Noah…" She said his name in a breathy voice, rough

with desire. She turned in his arms, facing him. "Don't stop, please."

He couldn't do this to her. "Ah, Lilly, do you know what you're asking?"

She kissed his jaw and then his neck. "Yes. I know."

Coop knew she wasn't thinking rationally, but neither was he. He wanted to blame it on not being with a woman in a long time. No, he'd never experienced anything like this. He'd never wanted a woman this badly, but he couldn't treat her as if she were a convenience. Lilly was too special.

The last of his common sense prevailed, bringing him back to reality. He had a job to do, and making love to the informant's widow wasn't part of it.

He tore his mouth away. "Lilly, you have to know I want you very much, but we haven't known each other for very long. My stay here in town is only for a few months."

"I'm not asking you for anything permanent, Noah." She stiffened and tried to pull away.

He refused to let her go. "I know that, Lilly, but you're the kind of woman who should expect that."

"I don't dream those dreams anymore." Her light green gaze lifted to his, her hand on his pounding heart. Could she feel the effect she had on him? "So you don't want me?"

He nearly laughed out loud. "I want you more than I can describe, but...this isn't what you want. I just didn't expect this... It's intense."

He placed a tender kiss on her lips and pressed her head back to his chest. He was stealing some time, but it was all he could have with this woman. A few stolen moments. And for the first time, he discovered he wanted so much more.

* * *

The sunlight streamed through the window as Lilly raised her head from the pillow. What happened? She got the answer quickly as her mind cleared and she remembered last night and being in Noah's arms.

Groaning, she dropped back onto the bed. She'd made a fool of herself, practically begging him to make love to her. Of course he turned her down. How pathetic was she? Yet, she allowed herself to conjure up images of Noah Cooper. Shirtless, with those low riding Levi's he wore… She grew breathless thinking about his lips moving over hers.

"The man can kiss." She recalled how his mouth had devoured hers, then he'd sent her to the house and to bed alone.

Her body grew hot. She'd never gone after a man before. Mike had been her only boyfriend, her only lover, and that was until college. She'd been a late bloomer. A nerd. A skinny girl in glasses who only cared about getting good grades. Now at thirty-four, she couldn't think about anything except a handsome carpenter, and how he made her feel amazing things.

There were so many other problems in her life. Her kids, her crazy ex-sister-in-law looking for God knows what. She thought about Noah again. How much he'd helped her.

Glancing at the clock, she knew if she didn't get up, her mother would come looking for her. She headed for the shower and fifteen minutes later she came downstairs to find the kitchen empty. On the counter was a note. Her mother had gone to church with Sean and they would pick up the kids from their sleepovers.

Lilly looked toward the cottage, knowing that a lot had changed since yesterday. How would Noah be today? Would he act differently toward her? It was after eight o'clock. Would he be coming to breakfast? She opened the back door to see that his truck was gone.

The disappointment hit her hard.

First thing that morning, Coop had put in a call to his captain, filling him in on what had happened at the Perry house.

Next was to keep the sheriff informed about what was going on. Coop made the second call and met Bradshaw at the edge of the construction site. If they were caught together, it could be easily explained.

The middle-aged sheriff was friendly but guarded. "Mornin', Coop. You wanted to talk to me?"

He explained what happened yesterday with Santos, then last night at the Perry house.

Brad leaned against his patrol car. "Damn. I don't like this." He shook his head. "Do you have any ideas where else to look for these papers?"

Coop adjusted his hat. "No. And I'm worried about Lilly Perry. Stephanie keeps insisting she's keeping Mike's things from her. She hasn't exactly been friendly about it, either."

The sheriff tugged his pants up over his rounded stomach. "This may be your expertise, Ranger Cooper, but this is my town. My first concern are the citizens. So don't be playin' hero. Call for backup if need be."

"That's my objective, too, Sheriff. To keep everyone safe." He stood straighter, but he also knew the ruthless drug lord he was dealing with. "But getting Delgado is our main focus. FYI, he's not going to make it easy for us."

No one wanted him worse than Coop did. The man was responsible for his brother's death, and more than likely he was responsible for Mike Perry's death, too.

"What should my men and I do then?"

"Keep an eye on the Dark Moon Arcade. It's a gut feeling, but I think something is going to happen there. And soon."

It was nearly lunchtime when Coop returned to the Staley house. He had to face Lilly, and he didn't want to see her disappointment. He cared too much to lead her on. She'd be upset anyway when she learned why he was really here.

He'd been undercover for the past two years, working every angle, hoping to get a chance at Delgado. If this one panned out, then he could go back to regular duty. Have a normal life again back in El Paso. He thought about his home. It had been an apartment close to the Ranger company office.

At thirty-seven, he couldn't even say he had put down roots. Not that he'd ever wanted to before. He drove into the Staleys' driveway and glanced at the grand Victorian house and the generations of family who'd lived here.

He thought about Lilly. She deserved a man to give her stability. Someone in this town. Someone who'd help raise her kids. He knew nothing about being a parent. His mother was preoccupied and his father had never showed up at all.

No. When he finished here, he'd leave and take another assignment, just like he always did. It was safer that way not to get involved. He wasn't even sure he could settle down in one place.

He parked and climbed out just as Robbie ran out of the house. "Hi, Coop. You want to play catch with me?"

Coop smiled. "Sure. Just let me talk to your mom for a second. Is she home?"

"Yeah, she's in the kitchen." The boy wrinkled up his nose. "I don't think she's very happy."

"Why is that?"

"'Cause when I talked to her, she wasn't listening."

"Maybe she's tired."

He shrugged. "Maybe you can make her happy."

Coop tugged on the boy's baseball cap. "I'll try."

He watched Robbie run off, then he knocked and walked into the kitchen. He found Lilly at the table with a notepad. She glanced up at him, and it was like a punch in the gut. Damn, if she didn't have that effect on him.

"You have a minute to talk?" he asked.

Lilly hesitated. She wanted to act as if nothing had happened, but it wasn't working. "Okay."

Noah walked in and Lilly got a funny feeling in her stomach. She had to stop acting this way. Noah Cooper was not the man for her. He'd told her that clearly enough last night.

His voice drew her attention. "I'm worried that last night wasn't a one-shot deal with Santos and Stephanie. How far are they willing to go to find these missing papers? What if they come to this house?"

Her eyes widened. "Here? You mean like break into my mother's house?"

He nodded. "They've approached you several times already. Could there be some of Mike's things mixed up with yours?"

She thought about it. "I left so much furniture at the house. I only took the beds and dressers. The kids' personal things, of course. Since Mike handled the finances..." That had been her mistake. "So I pretty much left all the papers with him. I always kept any job-related things separate from any of the landscaping business. Since I had custody of the kids, I took all their papers."

"Would you mind if I asked what they are?"

"A life insurance policy, birth certificates and my divorce papers."

She glanced down at the notepad. "That's what I've been doing here, making a list of places Mike's so-called papers could possibly be."

He seemed interested. "What did you come up with?"

"Of course, they're long shots. All my stuff I didn't want to go through went up to the attic. It's mostly pictures. I didn't want to bombard my mother with twelve years of things from my marriage. And a lot was thrown out."

She hated that she had to share her personal failings with this man. "Why do I feel like I'm in the middle of a nightmare, and I can't wake up?"

"I wish I could do more to help you," he told her. "But while I'm here I promise I'll do my best to keep Santos away from you and the kids."

Lilly was suddenly faced with the realization that Noah wouldn't always be around. But there was something else. Even though she didn't want to question his generosity, she couldn't help wonder about his interest in her problems.

"I can't depend on you for my safety." She had no idea what to do to get Stephanie to leave her alone. Then it came to her. "Or I'll just have to beat Stephanie to it, and find those papers myself."

CHAPTER NINE

LATER that evening, Coop stood inside the dark cottage and waited until he saw Lilly's bedroom light go out. He'd managed to talk her out of doing anything crazy. For now. But how long would that last? She was asking too many questions, and he couldn't answer them. Not without blowing his cover.

After lacing his running shoes, he headed for the door. It was safe to go out now. Not only was it a good cover so he could meet his contact, but it helped relieve stress, especially with Lilly talking about confronting Stephanie.

After a quick series of stretches, he started jogging down the driveway and headed north toward the edge of town, three miles to Perry's Landscaping. He was to meet up with a federal agent, Rico Vega, halfway there. Vega worked undercover as a day laborer and he'd been hired on the landscape crew for Vista Verde.

Coop picked up his pace as the adrenaline surged through him, unable to keep Lilly out of his head. He'd known he'd overstepped when it came to her. He never should have touched her. The way she made him feel was something he'd never allowed himself to think about.

Until now. When a certain blonde, green-eyed woman got under his skin. He felt the warning signal go off.

Yet, he couldn't seem to help himself when it came to

elementary school principal Lilly Perry. Surprisingly she wasn't even his type. He'd stayed far away from women who wanted a commitment, who came with kids.

He'd directed all his energy into getting the drug dealer who'd managed to slip away from the authorities on both sides of the border. They'd only been able to catch his lap-dogs, never the head guy. Santos, or Delgado—whatever he called himself.

Coop blew out a breath in frustration and turned the corner, heading toward the designated spot. He had to get the guy this time. A man lost his wife and his family trying to do the right thing and protect them. Like his brother, Devin, Perry's life needed to stand for something. Something to make his kids proud.

Again he thought about Lilly. She deserved to know the real man she'd been married to, and that Mike didn't leave her because he didn't love her but because he'd loved her enough to do what was right. To keep his family safe.

Coop slowed his pace as he approached a vacant building. This time of night the street was deserted, but that didn't allow Coop to let his guard down. He glanced around the darkness. Bad things happened even in a perfect small town like Kerry Springs.

Right before the corner, Coop saw the shadowed figure leaning against a doorway. He glanced around once again, then stopped and rested against the building's facade.

"Vega."

The man nodded. "Coop. Good to see you, *amigo.*"

The man pushed open the door and stepped inside the gutted storefront. There was just enough moonlight coming through the window for them to see each other.

He'd worked with Vega off and on with this investigation. "Tell me you got something for me," Coop said.

"Wouldn't that be nice? Make our job easy for a change." Vega sighed. "We might have a slight break this time. I've heard there's a delivery coming in at the end of the week. They say it's special fertilizer for Vista Verde."

"What makes you think it isn't just that?"

"Santos himself is going to be there. From what I learned from one of the workers, there are about four men who get to hang with Santos. They're the ones supervising this delivery."

"Do you know the time?"

Vega shook his head. "No. Just that the shipment is due by the end of the week. If it shows up, we're supposed to let the boss know ASAP." Vega pulled out a cigarette but didn't light it. "You have any info?"

Coop shook his head. He told him about Lilly's idea to search for the missing papers. "I'm worried about her and the kids' safety," he added.

Vega cursed in Spanish. He knew the history of Mike Perry. "I guess you've got your hands full with her." He released a breath. "I've already alerted my superior about the delivery. But we'll need backup. We can't risk losing this guy again." The agent paused. "There's another bit of info I received before I came here. Delgado was spotted in Laredo yesterday."

Coop froze. "They're sure it was him?"

"As sure as we can be."

"Damn. Why can't this be easy for once?" Coop shook his head. "I'll see you at the construction site tomorrow."

"Be careful," Vega warned. "I saw Santos work over one of his men yesterday. He enjoyed it too much."

Coop wasn't worried about himself, only Lilly and the family. If she had something Santos wanted, that put her in danger.

* * *

Coop made it back to the cottage in record time. He didn't like Lilly being alone. What would happen tomorrow when she was home all day by herself? And there were Kasey and Robbie. He needed to talk with Bradshaw again. Maybe he could get at least some extra patrols to come by the house.

He headed for his door as he stripped off his T-shirt, only wanting a shower and a few hours sleep. He stopped when he saw Lilly sitting on the back stoop.

"Lilly, is something wrong?"

She shook her head. "I just couldn't sleep." She stood and walked toward him, wearing a tank top and shorts, covered partly by a cotton robe that was loosely tied at her waist. "And by the looks of things, you couldn't, either."

He knew he had to back away, but he was frozen to the spot. Then she put her hand on his chest. He felt a different kind of burn and all rational thoughts went right out of his head.

"I usually run at night," he said weakly. "So I can sleep better."

She nodded, and finally looked up toward his face. "I went to the attic, and I found some boxes. I was wrong, there are some of Mike's things in them. I guess when we moved out of the house, things got mixed together."

"Are they papers?"

She nodded.

"Did you go through them?"

She shook her head. "I was afraid of what I might find. Would you go through them with me?"

"Of course." He didn't want to appear too anxious, but if there was even a chance of finding something against Santos…

"I can't sleep until I know what's there."

He slipped on his shirt. "What if it's nothing?"

"Then I will gladly hand everything over to Stephanie."

What he wouldn't give for a break on this case. "Then let's go."

"One box is on the porch. I didn't want the kids or my mother to know what's going on." She glanced away. "Would you mind if we went through it at the cottage?"

"No." Coop went to the porch and retrieved a large box, then carried it inside. Lilly followed him and he placed the overflowing box on the coffee table.

Lilly looked at him. "I'm not sure where this box came from but from what I see on top, it's probably just some old bills, tax returns and some statements from our joint bank account. It's probably a long shot."

"Hey, it's a shot." He didn't hesitate and began digging through the stack. She'd been right. Utility and department store bills, receipts, even a few greeting cards.

Lilly sat down and started sorting. She picked up a card that first brought a smile, remembering the Mother's Day card Kasey had made in school, then sadness followed.

"Lilly? Are you okay?"

She wiped a tear away and nodded. "Just some memories of my sweet little girl." She set it aside. "Maybe I should show her this and she might treat me a little nicer."

She didn't want to relive her the past, so she started digging out another stack of papers. Several were billing statements with the letterhead of a company, Collier Shipping. The amount was for over ten thousand dollars. On the bottom was a handwritten note. "Talk to S. about this."

"Noah, it's probably nothing but…" She handed it to him. "I never worked in the landscape office, so I'm not sure what this is."

Noah looked it over, frowning. "You don't know Collier Shipping?"

"They aren't local," she told him. "But I think 'S' stands for Stephanie."

"It's dated June nearly two years ago." He looked at her. "How long has Santos worked here?"

She frowned. "About two years. Mike mentioned some guy Stephanie was dating. School wasn't out yet." She swallowed. "That summer Mike and I started having trouble."

She stood as Noah continued digging through the box. "There are several more statements from Collier," he said. "Fifteen thousand, and this one is for almost thirty. Whatever they shipped was expensive."

"Plants and fertilizer? They started up the greenhouse and nursery that year."

Noah nodded, but continued going through the numerous papers. He had other ideas what the money was used for. "Every week? That's a lot of inventory for a small business. And why would Mike circle them in red ink?"

"I don't know. Do you think these papers are what Stephanie is looking for?"

Coop frowned. "She said they wanted tax papers. These were expenditures. And if there was illegal money coming in, they wouldn't want the IRS to know about it."

"Mike wouldn't do that," Lilly insisted. "He was an accountant and an honest man. At least he used to be."

Noah wanted to tell her the truth, but he didn't know it all himself. "Let's finish going through this before we make any judgments." He still needed proof. None of this made Santos guilty of anything. "And I'd make copies before giving the originals to Stephanie."

"So you think Santos and Stephanie are doing something illegal? What?" Her last guess came out a whisper. "Drugs?"

He hesitated a moment. "It doesn't matter what I think."

She studied him. "It does to me. If Stephanie is after this, then all I care about is keeping my family safe."

He took a step closer. "That's my first concern, too."

After gathering the two dozen receipts from the box, they walked across the backyard and into the house. No twenty-four-hour copy places were available in Kerry Springs, so the best Lilly had was the copier on the fax machine in the den.

With everyone in the house asleep, Noah shut the door, then closed the blinds before he let Lilly turn on the desk lamp. The computer was in the corner and she went right to work.

Coop knew there wasn't any proof of anything. But it was a start that might lead them to more. Could these deliveries be connected to drugs and money laundering?

Lilly sighed. "I still have trouble believing that Mike got involved in something illegal."

"What if he didn't have a choice?"

She looked confused then her eyes widened. "Oh, God! It was Stephanie who got him involved. Her and Santos."

"We don't know that, Lilly. This isn't enough evidence."

She stared at him, then said. "I'm sorry to pull you into this. Maybe I should go to the sheriff."

"And tell him what? There isn't enough with only this." He took the chance. "You said there were more boxes."

She nodded. "There are two more upstairs. It's pictures."

"Do you mind if we take a look?"

Lilly finished with the copies and left the papers on the desk.

They went up to the second floor, past the bedrooms to the end of the hall. Opening a door, she turned on a light that revealed bare wooden steps that led them to a large area with open rafters for the ceiling. She took him to a spot where there was furniture and stacked cartons.

She opened a box where there were photos on top. He couldn't help but glance over the family pictures. The kids were at different stages of growth. He stared at a very young bride and her groom. And Lilly couldn't have been very old, barely out of her teens.

"We were both still in college and didn't want to wait until after graduation. Our parents were afraid that we'd quit school, but we didn't." He watched a sad smile cross her face. "I might have been five months pregnant, but I graduated."

Coop wondered what it was like to care about someone so much that he couldn't wait to be with them. He looked at Lilly. "He must have loved you a lot." He found he was envious of what Mike and Lilly had together. "Some people never find anyone."

She smiled but there was sadness in her voice. "I thought we had it all. Then in a few short years everything changed. The business became his main focus. Sometimes it felt like I was married to a stranger."

"Maybe we'll find the reason why in here." Coop began to dig through the box, just so he wouldn't keep looking at Lilly and wondering what it would be like to have her in his life.

He was too aware of her presence. Too aware of what she felt like in his arms. He inhaled her scent and remembered what her kisses were like. He straightened. What he needed to realize was she wasn't his, and never would be.

This was a job, and that was all he needed to remember.

The next morning came far too soon. Lilly had been up early to fix breakfast for Noah. She knew he hadn't gotten much sleep, either, and he had to go to work at the construction site today. After they'd sat upstairs and gone through every single box and dresser drawer in the attic but they'd come up with nothing more. So he'd finally gone back to the cottage.

She'd wanted to stop Noah from leaving. There was no doubt in her mind she'd developed feelings for him. She was crazy to even think of anything permanent between them.

What if he stayed in Kerry Springs? What if he was beginning to care about her, too? Could she risk her heart again? It was already too late; she had already fallen for the man.

She heard the back door open and put on a smile as Noah walked in. He looked as if he'd just showered and shaved and he took her breath away.

"What are you doing up?" he asked. "I told you I'd stop by for coffee. I can grab something on the way to the site."

"It's all ready." She held up a plate of scrambled eggs and a slice of ham.

"Okay, I'm not going to turn this down." He straddled the stool at the counter. "Thank you, Lilly. Are you going to join me?"

She grabbed her coffee mug and sat down. "I'll keep you company."

Noah attacked his food and she enjoyed watching a man with an appetite. He glanced at her and winked. "What are your plans today?"

"Well, Robbie will be bored because you're gone. Kasey will be pouting. So I thought I'd take them to the library for some books."

"Always the teacher, huh?"

"I guess. Will you be working all day?" She rushed on to say, "I mean, will you be home for supper?" Even that sounded like she was checking up on him. "What I mean to say, should I expect you for supper?"

He smiled. "Yes, I'll be home after work, but don't cook because of me. In fact, why don't I take everyone out to eat tonight? You've been cooking all my meals. It's time I treated you all. We'll celebrate my first day at work."

She was surprised. "Oh, Noah, you don't have to do that."

"I wouldn't ask if I didn't want to. How about if we go to Rory's Bar and Grill?" Coop suggested.

"It's a date." She gasped, "I didn't mean it that way. I meant as a get-together. Not like you and me together."

He grinned. "It's okay, Lilly. I know what you meant." He glanced at the clock. "I better get going." After finishing his coffee, Noah walked to the door. He paused and looked back at her. With a smile he came back to her. "I probably shouldn't do this." He leaned down, cupped her face and kissed her.

"Stay out of trouble today. I'll see you tonight."

CHAPTER TEN

IT WAS nearly six o'clock and Lilly still hadn't been able to decide what to wear. It was a casual date. No, this wasn't even a date. It was supper with the kids and her mother and Noah. So why was she nervous?

She walked back into the closet and found her best pair of jeans and slipped them on. With a glance in the mirror, she nodded with approval. Not bad for almost thirty-five. She'd lost some weight and her rear end was still firm. Thank you, workout video.

She put on a silky, royal blue blouse and tucked it into her pants, then added a silver chain belt. She stepped into her strappy sandals with the small heels, adding two inches to her five-foot-eight height. Of course that wouldn't bother Noah Cooper since he was over six feet tall. She applied some lip gloss and ran a brush through her hair, then headed downstairs.

Lilly heard voices as she approached the kitchen where she found her mother, Robbie and Kasey talking with Coop.

She stood back and watched the interaction. Noah had managed to get Kasey to talk, and even coaxed a smile from her. Winning over Robbie hadn't been a problem, but her mother was different. She'd never had much of a relationship with Mike, especially since the way things ended.

Beth Staley was smiling now, so it seemed she didn't disapprove of anything about Noah.

Lilly didn't, either. "Hi, I didn't mean to keep everyone waiting," she said, sounding a little breathless. Maybe that was because she saw Noah's appreciative look.

He'd showered and changed into nice jeans and a collared shirt. "It was worth it," he told her.

"Yeah, Mom, you look pretty," Robbie echoed. "Now can we go eat?"

"Sure."

"Rory's, right?" her son cheered as Kasey agreed.

She wasn't surprised when everyone cheered.

"Barbecue sounds perfect," her mother said. She was dressed in a pretty rose-colored blouse and capri pants.

It only took about ten minutes until they arrived at Rory's Bar and Grill. Coop sized up the friendly crowd as they waited by the door to be seated. The place was in between a dated sports bar and family restaurant. There were several booths that lined the walls, along with some tables scattered around filled with loud, happy customers. A large oak bar that took up an entire wall had several female patrons lined up as the big Irishman served up the drinks with a smile. Beside Sean was his son Matt doing the same.

"Look, Grandma, there's Sean," Robbie said. Just then the man in question glanced up. A grin spread across his face as he came around the bar. Wiping his hands on his white bar apron, he walked toward them.

"Well, this is a pleasant surprise." He bent down and kissed Beth and Lilly, then hugged both kids. "Hello, Coop." He shook his hand. "What brings you all in tonight?"

"It's Coop's first day at work," Robbie offered. "We're celebrating."

"No, he's just tired of my cooking," Lilly said and they all laughed.

This was new to Coop, being with a family. "I thought everyone needed a change," he added. "It's too hot to cook anyway."

"Well, whatever reason," Sean told them, "I'm glad you're here. Let me find you a table." He glanced around to see the busboy clearing a booth and led them over. Once they were seated, he took their drink order.

Lilly nodded toward the bar. "Rory's seems to be a popular place tonight with the ladies."

Her comment had Sean grinning again. "It's Matt who brings them in. The lad always did have a way with the lasses."

Beth smiled right back at him. "I wonder where he inherited all that charm."

The big man leaned down and lowered his voice. "I only want to charm one." Then he placed a soft kiss on Beth Staley's cheek. "I'll be back with your drinks." He walked off.

"Oh, Grandma," Kasey breathed. "Sean is so sweet."

"I think so, too," the older woman echoed.

Coop looked at Lilly. She, too, seemed to be taken by the man. Great. How could he compete with that? Whoa. What was he thinking? That was the problem. He didn't need to be charming any woman. No matter how pretty she looked in blue, or how those killer legs of hers looked in jeans, he had dozens of reasons why he should stay clear of her. None of which he'd listened to. None of which stopped his growing desire for her. Somehow he needed to find a way.

A few minutes later the drinks arrived and after Sean took their order, he went back to the kitchen. For a little while, Coop just wanted to sit back and pretend that he could enjoy tonight. Tomorrow was soon enough to think about work. Didn't he get a little time off for himself?

Someone put money in the jukebox and a country-and-western song began to play. He stood and reached out for Beth's hand. "Mrs. Staley, would you care to dance?"

She blushed and stood. He escorted her out and they began to circle the floor with several other couples. "If you're trying to make Sean jealous it won't work. He knows how I feel about him."

"Doesn't hurt to keep him on his toes." He swung her around. "Pretty light on your feet, Miss Beth."

"You're not so bad yourself, Mr. Cooper."

He took her through a series of turns and they both laughed when they completed it without a hitch. "Well, would you look at that? Seems your daughter is trying to steal your man."

They both smiled when Sean came dancing by with Lilly in his arms. "I've got to put a stop to that," she said. "Dance over there."

The two couples ended up side by side. "Seems you have my lass," Sean said.

Beth went into Sean's arms, and Lilly came willingly into his, just as the music changed to a ballad. Coop wrapped his arm around her and pulled her close. They began to move to the seductive music and he breathed in the scent of her hair, her softness against him as her breasts brushed against his chest.

He knew this was all wrong, but he couldn't help himself when it came to Lilly Perry. It didn't matter how many times he told himself no, he still wanted her.

Lilly didn't want the night to end. It had been a long time since she felt this way. Even in the truck, she wished that it was only her and Noah riding back to the house. She thought back to the way he danced with her, holding her so close. How he made her want things she hadn't wanted in so long.

They pulled up at the house and everyone got out. The kids were chattering back and forth, and for once, not fighting. She hadn't seen her daughter this happy in a long time. Sean even got her to dance, and Noah took a turn, too. This was the first time in a long while that Kasey seemed happy. It was a perfect night. A night she didn't want to end by saying good-night to Noah.

Her mother followed behind the kids. "I'll put Robbie to bed. Why don't you two sit out here and enjoy the evening breeze?"

Once everyone was inside and Lilly and Noah were alone, he looked at her. "I should get to bed, too, since I need to be up early." He stepped toward her, cupping her face in his warm hands.

Lilly felt a shiver rush down her spine as he lowered his head and brushed his lips against hers. "Had a nice time," he whispered.

Lilly smiled. "So did I."

He touched her mouth again, teasing her as he nibbled on her lips before he pulled back. "Especially the dancing. You're not bad for a school principal."

"And you're not bad for a carpenter."

He started to lower his head again, then there was a shout from the house. Her mother rushed out the back door. "Coop, Lilly, someone broke into the house."

Coop ran into the house without hesitation. Nothing was amiss in the kitchen, or the living room, but the den was a different story. There were papers scattered everywhere, and the desk drawers were pulled out.

Lilly started to rush in, but he stopped her. "Don't touch anything. I've got to call the sheriff."

"Who would do this?" she said absently. "We don't have anything valuable." She looked at him and her eyes slowly widened. "Stephanie?"

He shook his head. That was his guess, but he couldn't say anything. He pulled his phone out and called Bradshaw. When he hung up, he heard the kids yelling.

"Mom," Robbie yelled and they hurried out into the hall as he came halfway down the steps and leaned over the banister. "Somebody messed up my room."

"Mom! Mom!" Kasey charged down, too, tears filling her eyes. "My room is torn apart, and so is yours."

While Lilly comforted her kids, Coop took the steps two at a time and went from one bedroom to the other. The beds were stripped, dresser drawers open and clothes tossed. Kasey came in with her mother. "Is anything missing?" he asked the teenager.

"I don't know, but my CDs and computer are gone." Coop looked over the girl's head to Lilly. He didn't need to say Stephanie's and Santos's names again.

"The insurance will replace everything, honey," Lilly told her daughter.

"But I had pictures…of Dad." A tear fell. "It was just him and me."

Lilly hugged her daughter. "Maybe we can find some more pictures."

Just then there was a flashing red light through the window as the sheriff's car pulled up out front.

"I'll go talk to Bradshaw." Coop looked at Robbie. "Don't touch anything in your room. Okay?"

The boy looked frightened.

He gave him a smile. "Hey, it's going to be okay."

Robbie followed him out into the hall and grabbed hold of his arm. "Coop, what if they come back when I'm sleeping?"

He found himself hugging the boy. It tore at him that a creep like Santos could frighten young kids like this. Somehow he'd find a way to stop him. "I won't let anything happen to you, or Kasey, Grandma Beth or your mom. And I'll stay here to make sure they don't."

The boy looked doubtful.

"I promise, Rob. I would never let anything happen to you. Now, I need to go and talk to the sheriff so he can catch who did this."

The boy finally let him go. "Okay."

Coop hurried downstairs to find Sheriff Bradshaw talking with Beth. "Beth, would you bring the family out here? I'll go inside and have a look around."

She nodded. "Coop, will you talk with the sheriff?"

"Sure." He started inside when Lilly came through the door with the kids. "Why don't you sit down? I'll show the sheriff the damage. Lilly, what did you do with those papers?"

"They're in my briefcase." She looked as frightened as her children. "It's in the car." She then walked toward the porch swing.

Coop led the sheriff into the den and they looked around at the destruction. "Seems they're getting desperate," he told Bradshaw in a low voice. "Whatever they want must be worth a lot."

"Then you better find it," the sheriff said as they walked back out to the porch. "I'll take prints, but I doubt we'll find anything."

So did Coop.

"Does the family have somewhere to stay with tonight? I won't be able to get a crew in until tomorrow."

"I'll find them a place."

Just then a truck pulled up and Sean Rafferty jumped out and hurried toward the house. "Is everyone all right?"

"Yes. They're just a little shaken."

"Praise be." He looked heavenward. "Where's Beth?"

He nodded toward the swing. "They can't stay here tonight."

"Of course not, they'll come to the ranch with me." He took off toward the group. He hugged Beth, then went down the line until he assured every family member that he'd take care of them.

Coop found he was envious that he couldn't do the same. What he needed to do right now was think about what Santos planned next. He could use some help. Dammit, Perry, where did you hide the proof?

Robbie ran to him. "I don't want to go with Sean, Coop. I want to stay with you. You said I could."

He looked at Lilly as she approached. "You and the kids are welcome to stay in the cottage."

"What about you?" she asked. "You have to work tomorrow."

"I'm sure Alex would understand."

Kasey walked up to them. "Mom, Grandma's getting some clean clothes from the laundry room. They're ready to go."

"I'm not going," Robbie said. "Coop said he wouldn't let the bad guys get me, so I'm staying here."

"Well, I'm not," Kasey added and marched off to Sean's truck.

Lilly looked at her frightened son, then back at Coop. "Could you handle two houseguests?"

This wasn't a good idea.

The lights were dim as Coop stood in the shadows and gazed out the cottage window toward the Staley house. The sheriff had left an hour ago, but there was a patrol car driving by every fifteen minutes or so.

He knew Santos wouldn't be back. Not tonight. Hell, this break-in was more of a warning than anything else. And if he could only find what they were looking for before they did this game would be over. Santos/Delgado would be in jail.

That was another thing. He couldn't let the drug lord panic and disappear over the border where they'd never find him. As it was, this guy had ways to move around at will.

Coop had contacted Vega earlier and he'd told him that Santos had been at the construction site, then went back to the landscape office the rest of the evening. Of course, that didn't mean he hadn't had someone else do his dirty work.

Now, all Coop had to do was figure out their next move. There was a delivery of drugs coming to Kerry Springs. He doubted it would have been the first, either. Was this the reason Mike Perry had to die? He figured out the operation. What about Stephanie? Did she care that little about her own brother that she let her so-called boyfriend take over?

"Noah?"

He turned around to see Lilly. He tried to remain reserved, controlled. She was wearing her usual sleeping attire: a tank top and a pair of cutoff knit shorts that exposed far too much leg. He blew out a breath. This was going to be a long night.

"How's Robbie?"

"Sound asleep. Lucky him, he's always slept like a rock."

She crossed the room toward him. "Are you going to stand guard all night?"

He gave a nod. "I promised Robbie." He glanced at her.

"A line was crossed tonight, Lilly. They mean business and aren't stopping until they find what they want."

"If you want to scare me, you're doing a good job."

"I want you aware, Lilly. I don't want anything to happen to you or the kids."

Lilly liked having someone to lean on. It had been so long since she'd had any kind of support, or to have a man around to protect her. Yet, even knowing it was a bad idea to have these feelings, she couldn't shut off her desire for this man. The last thing she needed to do was start something with Noah Cooper. He'd told her already that he wasn't the kind to stay for the long haul.

"Thank you for all you've done. And I'm sorry you've gotten involved in my problems."

He looked at her. "None of this is your fault. You just happen to be in the way of what they want."

"But, Mike…"

"If your ex-husband was involved, he needed to keep you and the family safe."

And now it was Noah Cooper doing that job. Not her husband, but a stranger who she didn't know much about. "May I ask you something?"

He shrugged. "Might as well."

"Why haven't you ever settled down?"

At first she didn't think he was going to answer. "Who said I haven't?"

She was surprised. "Were you married?"

He shook his head. "Almost was, when I was young and stupid."

Lilly couldn't stop her eagerness to know this man. "Was she your high-school sweetheart?"

He snickered. "Most girls I knew back then I wouldn't call sweet. But yes, Angie was one of the nice ones. Too nice for me. I was pretty wild back then, but she was my soft spot. I couldn't seem to say no to her." He glanced at Lilly. "We came from the same rough El Paso neighborhood. We were going to run off and live happily ever after."

Lilly was in between being jealous and curious about this woman. "What happened?"

"She got a better offer. A four-year college scholarship."

"Why didn't you wait for her?"

He shook his head. "She got her chance to break away from her bad life. I broke up with her and sent her off. Then I joined the military. It was the best for both of us."

"She didn't want to leave you, did she?"

He shrugged. "We were too young and besides, I didn't want to get attached at eighteen."

She couldn't help but think about the boy who'd lost so much. No dad. A mother who had passed away. The recent death of his brother. "No one since?"

He turned to her and those dark eyes bore down on her. "What do you want to hear, Lilly? That you keep me up at night? That I can't think of anything else?"

She felt a warm rush go through her. "Every woman likes to hear those things."

"That's the problem, Lilly. You aren't any woman. You're the kind a man can't walk away from." He leaned toward her and she couldn't take a breath. "Even when he knows he should.

"You're that woman that every man dreams about," he went on, then brushed his lips over hers, once, twice and finally his hands cupped her face and held her there as his mouth moved over hers, feeling, tasting, caressing. When he finally broke off they were both breathing hard.

"We can't do this, Lilly."

"Then send me away," she told him as she rose up and kissed his jaw, then his neck. This was so out of character for her. She never went after a man, was never the aggressor. "But not if you want me."

Coop gripped Lilly by the arms, only meaning to move her away, instead he pulled her closer. With her gasp, his mouth covered hers. Just one more kiss, he told himself as he parted her lips and pressed his tongue inside. One more taste, he promised. Yet he already knew it would never be enough.

He finally broke off the kiss and tried once more. Yet— even with her son sleeping in the next room—he was praying she wouldn't reject him. "Lilly. It still isn't right."

Even in the shadowed light, he could see those haunting green eyes. "It's all right to want me, Noah."

"Oh, God. I want you like I've never wanted anything in my life. But—"

Her mouth covered his, stopping any more protest. "I want you, too, Noah," she breathed. "I don't want anything more from you tonight than to know that you desire me. To make the rest of the world go away."

He wrapped his arms around her and pulled her to the sofa. His mouth closed over hers as he lowered her to the cushions. He shut off everything from his head, and concentrated on Lilly. Nothing else mattered but being with her.

CHAPTER ELEVEN

THE next morning, Cooper took his post at the window, staring out at the sunrise, then glanced back at the sofa. It was empty now. He'd reluctantly sent Lilly into the bedroom hours ago. He wanted nothing more than to have her stay, to hold her during the night, to make love to her all over again. To make promises he had no right to make, but in his heart he wanted her like no other woman.

He couldn't do any of those things. He was a Texas Ranger, and for now, working a case. He couldn't be distracted by anyone or anything. Yet last night he'd crossed the line, and by making love to Lilly Perry he'd broken every rule in his book.

He closed his eyes. Not that he regretted a second of being with her, holding her, loving her. Ethically it was wrong, no matter how right it had felt to him, or how much he'd come to care for Lilly. He couldn't let this go any further. He had to keep her safe. Keep them all safe. And the only guarantee was to get Santos and put him away for a long time. Of course, once Lilly learned the truth, she would hate him.

"Coop…"

He swung around surprised to see a sleepy-looking boy. "Hey, Robbie. What are you doing up so early?"

He shrugged. "I don't know." He came toward him,

wearing a T-shirt and a pair of sweatpants. "Mom's still sleeping."

And he'd wished he was there next to her. "Good. She needs her rest. Are you hungry?"

The boy shook his head as a frown marred his face. "I have to tell you something."

"Okay, what is it?"

He looked up at him with those big blue eyes. "Promise you won't get mad."

"I won't get mad." He couldn't imagine what the kid could do to upset him. He crouched down in front of him. "What is it, son?"

Robbie brought his hand out from behind his back and Coop was relieved to see a baseball. "I sneaked this out of my bedroom when you said we shouldn't touch anything. I didn't want to lose it. The bad man broke the case and I found it on the floor. When my dad gave it to me, he said I had to take care of it." He shook his head. "I had to take it, 'cause I promised."

Coop looked down at the autographed Nolan Ryan baseball. "I think it's okay."

The boy didn't look relieved. "But something else happened to it, and I don't want Mom to blame me." He turned the ball over to show the stitching along one of the seams was opening up. "See, it's coming apart. Can you fix it, huh, Coop? Please."

Coop eyed it closely. The stuffing was coming out, too. That was odd. Then he realized that the ball looked strange. The covering wasn't as taut as it should be. Had someone tampered with it? "Why don't you let me have a look at it?"

The boy handed it over. That was when Coop realized how light the ball felt. "You go and get dressed. I promise

I'll take good care of this. And be quiet so you don't wake your mom."

"Okay." Robbie smiled. "Thanks." The boy walked off.

After the door closed, Coop took out his pocketknife. He had an odd hunch as he began cutting farther along the seam. He dug out the stuffing and realized the cork center was missing. In its place was a hard foam.

His hopes were still high. Could Perry have hidden something…? He worked carefully to pull the center out, and as he unwrapped the foam, and discovered a small object.

"Damn." It was a key. He had no doubt that Perry hid it inside his son's baseball.

He pocketed the key and began to replace the stuffing until he could have the ball fixed. He pulled out his cell phone and punched in his captain's number.

When Ben Collier answered, he said, "It's Coop. I believe I found the proof we need." He went on to explain about the baseball. "If this is what I think it is, Mike Perry probably got all the information we want in a safe-deposit box, or a locker."

"Okay, Coop," his captain said. "You hold tight, I'll have two Rangers there in a few hours. You are not to go after it on your own. I repeat, you're not to go on your own. Santos is probably watching you."

Coop felt excitement rush through him. "You're right. But I want to be there when we find the evidence."

The captain agreed, and Coop listened for more instructions. "I'll wait to hear about the meeting place." He flipped closed the phone and turned around to find Lilly standing there. He didn't have to ask if she heard, her expression told it all.

He put on a smile. "Good morning, Lilly."

She looked beautiful, but angry. "Who are you?"

He wasn't sure how much to say and keep her safe. "Noah Cooper."

"That's your real name?"

"Yes. I'm Noah Cooper."

"You're not a carpenter, are you?"

He started toward her, but stopped. "Lilly, I'm not able to tell you much right now. I don't want to put you in any more danger."

She forced a laugh. "Just tell me if you're the good guy or the bad guy."

He felt like a heel. "Good guy. You can ask Sheriff Bradshaw, but that's all I'm at liberty to say right now. Not until we finish this."

"You're talking about Stephanie and Rey Santos aren't you?"

He nodded. "And I can't say any more, except this is serious. We don't want anyone else hurt."

She couldn't hide the hurt on her face. He wished he could take it away.

"These weeks you've been staying here." Her voice was shaky. "It was all a lie?"

He went to her, grateful she didn't back away. "Give me twenty-four hours, Lilly. I'll tell you anything you want to know. I promise."

Those incredible green eyes searched his face. "Last night was a lie, part of an act."

He released a breath, knowing he had to be truthful about this. "No, Lilly, nothing between you and me was a lie."

An hour later at the cottage, Lilly had managed to get a shower. She'd cried through the streaming spray, but she didn't feel any better. Her life was in shambles. Her crazy sister-in-law was after her. Once again she'd been betrayed by a man, and in some ways it felt worse than when Mike had left her.

The only thing she really knew about Noah Cooper was that he was doing some sort of undercover operation, and getting in good with her and her family was part of his job. She thought about last night, and how she'd literally thrown herself at him, practically begging him to make love to her. Of course, he took what she offered.

Dear God, had she meant anything to him?

She managed to pull herself together, and get dressed in fresh clothes Noah had brought from the house. She added some makeup from her purse and checked herself in the mirror. She gathered her things up and saw Noah's personal items on the counter, reminding her that she had to face him again. She ran a brush through her hair, then pulled it back into a ponytail.

She released a breath, then walked into the living room to find Noah gone. Instead there was a woman sitting on the sofa with Robbie.

"Excuse me. Who are you?"

Robbie jumped off the sofa first. "Mom, this is Karen. She's a special agent. Isn't that cool? Coop had to leave, but he said I should trust Agent Karen to take care of us until he comes back."

The blond-haired woman looked to be about Lilly's age. "Hello, Mrs. Perry, I'm Federal Agent Karen Baker. And until this case is completed, I'm here for you and your son."

"What case?"

"I'm sorry, ma'am, I'm not at liberty to talk about it."

Robbie jumped in. "Coop said it has to be a secret for now."

It seemed that Noah had confided in her son more than her. She didn't like being in the dark, not when it came to her family's safety. "Is it okay if we go see my mother?

She's working at the Blind Stitch downtown. My daughter is with her."

"Just let me check." The agent took out her phone and made a call. Lilly couldn't help but wonder if she was talking to Noah.

Stop thinking about the man. Whenever this mess with Santos was over, she knew that Noah Cooper would be gone.

Karen Baker closed her phone and turned to her. "It should be fine. I do need to stay with you and your son."

"Whatever," Lilly snapped. She knew this woman was only doing her job, but that didn't mean she had to like it. "Sorry. It has been a trying few days."

Her son came to her. "It's okay, Mom. Coop's going to fix it."

Lilly felt tears threatening. Was he going to fix her broken heart, too? "Come on, let's go see Grandma and Kasey."

Agent Baker checked the outside area then led them to a black sedan. Once they arrived at the Blind Stitch, Lilly rushed her son through the doors, anxious to see her mother. She was with Kasey in the classroom area talking to the women of the Quilter's Corner. Her mother crossed the room as Lilly grabbed her in a hug, then she burst into tears.

"Honey, what's wrong?" her mother asked, pulling her farther away toward a private corner.

Lilly shook her head. "I wanted to make sure you and Kasey were safe. I'll be okay in a few minutes," she said, but couldn't stop her tears.

Her mother took her by her arm and started out of the room. "Kasey, would you watch your brother while I talk to your mom?"

It surprised Lilly that her daughter looked so concerned.

"It's going to be okay, Mom," Kasey said and hugged her. "Coop will help us."

Lilly nodded again and followed her mother through the back of the shop and up the stairs to an attic apartment. It was a nice little place. There was a kitchenette, a living area with a sofa and a flat screen television. Jenny had once lived here when she was single.

"Okay, now tell me what else happened since last night?"

Lilly couldn't tell her mother how she'd been a fool and jumped into bed with a man she barely knew. How she'd fallen in love, and he was going to leave her.

"Noah found a key." She shook her head. "I overheard a phone conversation, so I'm not exactly sure of all the details. But it has to do with this key and some information about Stephanie and Santos."

Her mother nodded. "Good, then we'll finally get to the bottom of this mess. And they'll get out of our lives."

"It's all so crazy. Mom, Noah lied to us. He's not a carpenter. He's working undercover for some government organization and he won't say which. He's been after Santos for a while, too."

Beth Staley smiled. "Well, I see a lot of things more clearly now. His interest in helping you find the papers." She looked at her daughter. "But you're upset because he didn't confide in you, that he didn't tell you about the operation."

It was a little more than that, she thought. The man didn't need to get involved with her.

"Lilly, if Noah was working undercover, he couldn't. It would have put us all in danger."

"But I thought he cared about me—us," she blurted.

Her mother studied her. "From what I saw, I'd say Noah

does care very much about you. And you care about him. So I'd say for that reason it made his job even harder."

Lilly shook her head. "How can I trust him?"

"Listen, daughter." Her mother gave her a stern look. "Don't you want the question about Mike cleared up? Don't you want to finally move on with your life and put all the past behind you and the kids?"

"Of course I do."

"Well, Noah Cooper is the one who might be able to do that."

"But it got…personal last night."

Her mother smiled. "Oh, is that what they call it these days?"

Lilly couldn't stop the heat creeping up her neck to her face.

"Look, Lilly, I can't tell you what to do any longer. Just give yourself some time, at least until this case is cleared up." She took her daughter's hand. "But if you're lucky enough to find love again, then don't let it slip away." She smiled. "I'm not."

"I might not be that lucky, Mom. I don't think it's up to me."

Cooper was losing patience as he and Vega climbed out of his truck. They'd been to two bus stations with nothing to show for it. They hadn't used the same kind of key. This one was a stubby key with a plastic base.

Where would Mike feel safe hiding the evidence? He could go ask Lilly, but she didn't know much about her ex's life the past year. He couldn't put her through an interrogation, no matter how easy he'd make it. No, he needed to rely on the other agents searching the surrounding area.

"Hey, let's grab something to eat," Vega suggested. "And then we'll start again."

"I'm not hungry."

"Well, I am." The agent nodded toward Rory's Bar and Grill. "C'mon, a quick sandwich."

After making a call, Coop followed him inside. He was surprised to find Sean working today. He followed Vega up to the bar as a flash of memories hit him, recalling being here with Lilly and the kids. How he danced with her. How she'd felt in his arms.

"Hey, Coop. How are you doin'?"

He blinked, hearing Sean's voice as he climbed onto a stool. "I've been better."

"I'd say you look as miserable as Lilly does. This mess with Stephanie and Santos is bad for everyone. Wish the sheriff could get rid of him."

"You said you saw Lilly."

"Yeah, they're all at the Blind Stitch."

Good, they were safe there, especially with Agent Baker.

"What can I get for you two?"

"Iced tea, and a barbecue sandwich."

"I'll just have iced tea."

Sean brought over the tea and he took a drink. "Hey, Sean," Coop asked. "Would you happen to know if there is anywhere in town you could find a locker with a removable key? You put in coins and you keep the key."

The gray-haired man leaned back against the counter. "Sure. The bus station still has them."

"Anywhere else?"

Sean raised an eyebrow. "There's the locker room at the fitness center." He reached into his pocket and pulled out his key. "I go there to swim."

Coop pulled his key out of his pocket and compared it to Sean's. They were identical. "Bingo."

Vega whispered something in Spanish.

"Where is this fitness center?" Coop asked as he pulled out his phone.

"Two blocks down, make a left and go three more blocks. It's on your left side."

Vega pulled out a five and left it on the counter. "Hey, hold the sandwiches," he called as they were out the door and followed his partner into the truck. "Are you going to be okay?" he asked.

"Yeah, I will be as soon as I get this guy."

For the first time in over two years, he thought he might be close. Coop tried not to drive too fast. He had to remain professional about this. Do his job, and not think about Lilly right now.

"This is personal for you, huh, *amigo*?" Vega glanced across the truck cab. "This *hombre* killed your brother."

Coop didn't want to go into details. "Delgado's responsible for a lot of deaths, maybe not all directly, but like my brother's, he'd ordered them. We just need to prove it. Dammit, he needs to be off the streets."

He pulled up out front of the building with the sign Kerry Springs Community Center and got out as the sheriff pulled up. Brad got out of the patrol car along with Captain Collier and a federal agent.

Without many formalities the foursome went inside. It was the sheriff who spoke to an older woman behind the counter.

She smiled and said. "You here to arrest someone, Brad?"

"Not unless you're causing trouble, Emma." He nodded. "We'd like to check the men's locker room."

She eyed the group, then said, "Sure. Just let me know if the guys are leaving their towels lying around."

They walked down the hall past the door to the inside gym. Coop felt the adrenaline flow with anticipation as they entered a room lined with small lockers. This had to be it. He took out the key and checked the number again.

"Which one, Coop?" his captain asked.

"One eighty-nine."

"Here it is," Vega called from the end of the row in the corner.

Slipping on rubber gloves, Coop walked up and inserted the key. It turned and the door opened. He pulled on the handle and swung it open, revealing a black gym bag. Coop took it out and set it on the bench, then stood back and drew a breath.

"You want me to do it?" his captain asked.

Coop nodded. He'd gotten too close to this. His brother, Lilly's husband. He wanted to end it. Now.

Collier unzipped the bag, and reached inside and found a towel, but below that was a thick manila envelope. The captain opened it and pulled out a stack of papers with a cover letter. Both Collier and the federal agent went over them for the next few minutes.

"It's from Michael Perry." He handed Coop the letter. Coop began to read to himself.

To whom this may concern:
I hope there is enough here to put Santos away for a long time. It was difficult to get everything because I was being watched 24/7. But when possible I made copies of all their activities. As much as I tried, I couldn't convince my sister, Stephanie Perry, to leave him. So the only thing I could do was act as if I went along with everything. I gave up my wife and family to secure their safety.

Perry went on to tell of places and times of deliveries. And the big surprise was that Santos and Delgado were two different people. They were twin brothers. It suddenly dawned on Coop that that had been the reason they could move so freely back and forth across the border.

The letter also told that the drug shipments were coming through Nuevo Laredo, packed in bags of fertilizer and in the base of plants. He gave the location of a warehouse, and the twin, Delgado's, headquarters.

Perry went on to talk about hiding a second set of papers to throw off Santos. He knew his days were numbered, and was hoping to get to the agents before he was discovered, or his family was put in any more danger. His main concern was that his wife and kids would be protected from Santos.

The letter was signed, Michael Perry, and dated two days before his death.

"Okay, I'd say we have enough to get him—or them, Santos and Delgado. So I need to alert border patrol."

His captain looked at him. "You want in on this, Ranger Cooper?"

Coop pulled his Texas Ranger badge out of his pocket and pinned it on his shirt. "Wouldn't miss it."

CHAPTER TWELVE

Hours later, Lilly was beginning to feel like a prisoner as she paced the small apartment over the Blind Stitch, but she knew she and the kids were safest here. Sean had sent over some food for them and Kasey and Robbie were watching a video on television. Restless, she went to the window. The street was busy with five o'clock traffic, as much as Kerry Springs had of it.

She couldn't help but wonder about Noah. What was he doing right now? Was he safe? Did he go after Santos and Stephanie? What had happened to her calm and easy life? Now she had a bodyguard and her family had been threatened.

And she'd fallen in love with a stranger.

A tear hit her cheek and she wiped it away. *Who are you, Noah Cooper?* She only knew he was one of the good guys.

"Mom!"

She turned at Kasey's voice. That's when she saw Stephanie Perry standing at the top of the stairs, holding a gun. Her kids hurried to her side and Lilly held them close. "Stephanie, what are you doing here?"

The big-boned woman looked worse than usual. "Don't act innocent. You found Mike's papers, didn't you?"

Had Noah found them? "I don't know what you're talking about, Stephanie."

"I saw the sheriff going out to the yard. Because of you, Rey left me."

"Maybe that's a good thing."

Her ex-sister-in-law glared. "You always did hate me because Mike gave me so much attention."

"Let's not bring Mike into this, Stephanie. He's gone and there's no reason to hurt her kids."

"Yeah, don't say nothing bad about my daddy," Robbie said bravely.

Stephanie glared, her eyes cold. "Everything would be fine if it weren't for your daddy, little boy." She looked at Lilly and waved her gun. "If he had just kept his mouth shut, there wouldn't be a problem." Tears filled her sister-in-law's eyes. "But he wouldn't listen to us. Rey couldn't take the chance that he'd go to the law. There wasn't a choice, Lilly, but at least I made it easy for him. He was asleep, and didn't even know what was going to happen. It was peaceful."

She took a step toward Lilly and she stepped back with her kids. Oh, God, Stephanie helped kill her own brother. She needed to get help.

"He was your brother, Stephanie." Lilly tried to keep her attention. "He loved you."

"And he didn't want me to have Rey. Rey was the first man to care about me. He loves me and I love him. We were going to run off to Mexico, but now you've spoiled everything. Rey's gone without me."

"Surely you can still go."

She took a step closer. "That's right. You and the kids need to drive me to Mexico."

Kasey whimpered. "Mom…"

"It's okay," she whispered and shielded her kids behind

her, trying to control her fear. "Stephanie, you can't take my kids. I'll go."

That was when she saw Noah making his way up the steps. He placed his finger over his lips to keep silent.

Before she could speak again, Noah made his move, grabbing Stephanie from behind and knocking the gun from her hands. She was pinned to the floor in seconds. Then the other agents came rushing up the stairs. Stephanie was cuffed and being read her Miranda rights, then was led off.

Coop tried to slow his breathing as he looked at Lilly. That had been way too close for comfort. "Are you guys all right?"

Both Kasey and Robbie ran to him and hugged his waist. "I was so scared," Kasey admitted. "If you hadn't gotten here in time…"

"I wasn't scared," Robbie said. "I knew you'd come and save us. You're a Texas Ranger. Wow!" He touched the star pinned to Noah's shirt. "That's cool."

"Sorry, I couldn't tell you before," Coop said to the boy. "I had to keep it a secret so I could get the bad guys. Thanks to your baseball and your dad, we did both."

His eyes widened. "Really?"

Again he looked at Lilly. "I'm sorry it took so long. We didn't know where Stephanie was until Santos told us. She came through the unlocked door from the alley. The agent was posted out front."

Beth hurried up the steps and hugged each grandchild and her daughter, then started downstairs with Kasey and Robbie. It was Coop who stopped Lilly.

"Could I speak with you?"

Lilly watched as her children disappeared down the stairs, the door closing behind them. The silence was deafening as they were left alone. Lilly finally turned back to

Noah. She looked over his uniform, white shirt with his five point star badge. "So you're a Texas Ranger?"

He nodded. "I work undercover a lot, out of El Paso. Homeland security called us in on this case."

She glanced away from him. "I should go be with the kids."

"This will only take a short time, Lilly. I want to let you know that we found the papers Rey Santos had been looking for."

She looked relieved. "You have him in custody?"

He nodded. "We've had the business under surveillance for a few weeks. So once we got the proof, and a warrant from a judge, we went to the landscape yard. Santos had just left, but we caught up with him about twenty miles out of town. Guess that's why Stephanie came here…he'd ditched her like excess baggage."

He released a breath. "We're leaving now to apprehend his brother, Delgado. We got a tip about where he crosses the border." He pushed his hat back. "It's thanks to your husband, Mike, that we have evidence. He was the one who contacted us about Santos's operation."

Tears formed in Lilly's eyes.

"Lilly, he only left you to protect you and the kids. Santos wouldn't let him walk away from the operation. So to keep you safe, he filed for divorce. He'd set up a meeting with federal agents, but they didn't get here in time. When they heard of Mike Perry's suicide, they had a feeling he was the informant. We're sorry we couldn't get there soon enough."

She nodded. "You did the best you could."

"Sometimes that's not good enough."

"So the reason you came here was to find the evidence?"

He nodded. "We've been after Delgado for a long time. He's been bringing drugs across the border for years.

Nothing we did could stop him." He stepped closer. "This information isn't for public knowledge, yet, but I felt you needed to know. You lost so much the past two years. It's the reason I couldn't tell you who I was. The reason I moved into the cottage. I figured it was the best way to protect you and the kids."

Lilly wasn't trying to block out his words, but they managed to cut deep.

"Look, Lilly, I know you're not ready to hear this, but I still have to tell you, I never planned to get personally involved with you. I only wanted you all safe, to protect you and the kids."

"Please, I prefer not to talk about last night."

Coop hesitated then nodded. He saw her pain and hurt, and hated himself for causing it. He pulled out a long envelope from his back pocket. "It's not the original letter, because that's in evidence, but this is a letter Mike wrote to you. He wanted to be sure you knew the real truth."

Her hand was shaking as he gave it to her. "Thank you."

"I don't want your thanks, Lilly. I handled this all wrong. The only good thing that happened is that we got a drug lord off the streets and hopefully in prison for the rest of his life. Stephanie is going there, too, so you don't have to worry any longer about her."

He heard Rico call his name from downstairs. "I need to head down to the border for Delgado."

She looked at him with those hazel eyes that would forever haunt him. His chest tightened at the thought of leaving her. "But I'm coming back, Lilly. We'll talk, and I'll tell you everything."

"Seems there's nothing left to talk about, Noah. Your job here seems to be finished."

He stood there for a long time, trying to find the words. He couldn't find them so instead he drew her into his arms and covered her mouth with his. The kiss was deep and all consuming. When he finally released her they were both breathless. "No, Lilly. We're not finished, not by a long shot."

Two days passed before Lilly, Beth and the kids were able to get back into the house. It had been cleaned and everything put back the way it was before. They were still pretty shaken up and they stuck pretty close together, unable to forget the events of the past few days.

Even knowing Santos and Stephanie were in jail, they couldn't help but be worried about staying alone. Sean spent the first few nights in the guest room.

With the house quiet, Lilly walked outside onto the porch and sat down on the swing. The evening air was warm, but tolerable. It felt good to be outside and feel safe again. She wanted so much to enjoy the rest of the summer, maybe take the kids on a short vacation. In a few weeks she had to go back to work to get ready for a new school year.

Her thoughts turned to Noah. Maybe it was good that he'd left town. She hadn't been around to see him gather up his things from the cottage, which was for the best. Besides, he was probably already on another job.

Great. Now she was worried about his safety.

No, she had to stop thinking about him. He was where he belonged, in El Paso. She belonged here in Kerry Springs. Two different worlds. Then why was it such a struggle to put the man out of her head, out of her heart? He'd told her that he wasn't the kind to settle down. He did undercover work, and she was a school principal and the mother of two kids. What kind of life would that be? Not that the man had offered her any future. Just because she'd spent a night in his arms, making love to him didn't give her any rights. Only guilt.

She saw a shadow and jumped. "Who's there?"

"It's me, Coop." He stepped onto the walkway so she could see him.

Oh, God. "What are you doing here?"

His expression didn't give anything away. "I just got back from Mexico."

"Did you find Delgado?"

"Yes. We got lucky and apprehended him as he crossed the border. He's in custody. I had to come back to town to finish up some things on the case. We've been out at Perry's Landscaping, collecting more evidence."

Coop couldn't stop looking at her. Lilly's beauty had always left him awestruck. His feelings for her hadn't changed, either. He was crazy about her and no matter what he did, she wouldn't get out of his head. "I had to stop by and see how you and the kids are doing."

She stood up. "As well as can be expected. They're in bed. I took them to the cemetery today. We've never been to Mike's graveside, not since the stone marker was placed there. I felt in light of what has happened, it was important for them to get closure. To let them know what their father did. How much he loved them. And if anything good came out of this tragedy, it's that."

He nodded, but he didn't come up the steps. He didn't trust his feelings, and Lilly wasn't ready for what he was wanting to offer her. "Tell Rob that as soon as they release his baseball from evidence, I'll get it repaired and back to him."

"You don't need to do that, Noah."

He lost the fight and walked up to the porch. "I like it when you call me by my name."

The streetlight illuminated the porch just enough. He

couldn't see her eye color, but he could see her reaction to him coming close to her. "But only when you say it, Lilly."

She released a shaky breath and turned away. "When will you be going back to El Paso?"

He wanted to say never, but he had a job to do. "Probably tomorrow."

She looked at him. "So soon. I mean, your work here is finished?"

So she didn't want him to leave. "No. This case will take a while to put together for the prosecution, so I'll be back and forth."

"Oh, I see," she said.

No, she didn't see anything. "Would that really bother you, Lilly? If I left? If I left for good?"

"I don't know how to answer that, Noah. These past few days, my entire life has been turned upside down. My kids, too. I can't think about anything except putting one foot in front of the other."

"Of course. Just so you know, I want to help, Lilly, but I won't push you." He took out a business card and handed it her. "Call me if you need anything, day or night." Unable to resist, he leaned down and brushed his mouth over hers. "I know you're not ready now, but I'm coming back."

Then the hardest thing he'd ever had to do was turn and walk away from Lilly Perry.

CHAPTER THIRTEEN

Two weeks later, Lilly drove downtown. It was hard to believe how fast the time had gone. Soon summer would be over, and it would be fall and a new school year. She'd return to work and the past few months would all be a memory.

At least she would stop thinking about the "what ifs" all the time.

What if she'd known what had been going on with Mike? What if she'd had a better relationship with her daughter? What if she'd never met and fallen in love with a Texas Ranger?

Lilly shook away the thoughts. As her mother had told her during a recent late night talk, *You can't go back in time. Get closure on the past and only then can you move forward and think of the future.*

That was Lilly's first priority, to help her children heal. Hers would come later when she could think objectively about Noah Cooper. Problem was she wasn't sure she ever could.

Putting on a smile, she walked into the Blind Stitch. Jenny had returned to work this week, so her mother was back hanging out with her friends at the Quilter's Corner.

Of course, the conversation these days was more about

a certain man, Sean Rafferty, rather than how many baby quilts they needed to make for the upcoming year.

Lilly sent a wave to Jenny behind the counter, then headed over to the corner table. She felt warmth from just being here, in this shop. Once the word broke about what happened with Stephanie and Santos, a lot of people wanted to help her. Her closest friends were these women here at the shop, Jenny, Millie, Allison and Liz and, of course, her mother.

She walked to the table to find the ladies putting together a beautiful wedding ring pattern. "Oh, my, this is so beautiful." She loved the soft greens and yellows and all the detail the ladies put into their work. They could easily sell them for hundreds of dollars, but they preferred to give them away as gifts. "Who's the lucky couple who's getting this one?"

Liz shrugged. "Not sure, yet. We just want to be ready if and when the time comes."

Lilly glanced around the table, but no one would look at her. Was it for her mother? She looked at Beth Staley. She was busy pinning fabric. Were she and Sean ready to take the next step? Did that mean he would move into the house in town?

If so, that meant Lilly and the kids needed to find a place to live. It was time, too. Maybe she could find an apartment, or a small house to rent, at least until she cleared up her finances. Whatever, she had to look into something, because she didn't want to delay her mother's happiness. And it was time for her to move on with her life, too.

She took a breath. "Well, does anyone want to go to lunch?"

"We don't need to go out today," Beth said. "Sean's sending over some sandwiches. We've been so busy with projects, we want to keep working. There's plenty if you want to stay."

"Sure. I'll go visit with Jenny and see little Mick."

"He's not so little anymore," her mother said, smiling. "I guess he takes after his grandfather."

"I'll go see for myself."

Lilly went to Jenny behind the counter. The baby was in the carrier, swinging his little fists at a dangling toy not far away. "Hey, big guy," she said, taking in his rounded face. Once rewarded with a slobbery grin, she glanced at Jenny. "He's gotten so big."

Jenny nodded. "It's hard to believe, isn't it? He's making sounds and trying to roll over. And he's awake a lot more." She unfastened her son from the carrier as the baby kicked his legs excitedly.

"I can't believe how much he looks like Evan," Lilly said as she took the little guy from Jenny.

"Be warned, he's probably hungry and he'll latch on to anything."

The baby grabbed Lilly's finger. "Oh, my, you sure have a strong grip, young man."

The bell over the door rang and Lilly glanced over her shoulder to see Noah standing across the room. Her breath caught in her chest, her throat suddenly went dry as her gaze moved over him. He was dressed in the standard Texas Ranger uniform, a white shirt, a tie and khaki pants. His badge was displayed on his broad chest and his gun at his waist. A tan Stetson partly covered his dark hair and in his hands was a box from Rory's.

He walked toward her. "Hi, Lilly."

The baby started wiggling in her arms. "What are you doing here?"

"Right now, I've been recruited to deliver lunch." He

raised the box, but his gaze remained on her face. "How have you been?"

"Fine." Little Mick squirmed and tried to root against her breast. She felt herself blush as she glanced back to see Noah still watching her.

Noah took a step closer and his voice lowered. "He seems to be hungry."

She felt a shiver from his intimate tone. "Well, that's something I can't help with." Her blush grew and she looked for Jenny as Mick let out a wail.

His mother suddenly appeared. "Here, let me have him." Jenny took him. "Thanks, Lilly." She glanced at Noah, but Mick's impatience didn't allow his mother time for any pleasantries. "Hi, Coop. Sorry, I can't visit, this guy wants to be fed." She took off toward the back of the shop with the crying baby.

"I guess it's pretty hard to juggle work and a baby."

"It can be done," Lilly said. "If you have someone helping, and Jenny does. Evan's great."

Those bedroom eyes locked on hers. "Do you miss not having babies, Lilly?" he asked.

Being an only child, she'd always wanted a big family. "Sometimes. That happens when a woman is getting older." She didn't want to talk babies with Noah. "What are you doing back in town?"

"There's a lot to finish up on the investigation."

"I guess so." She was uncomfortable with this. She didn't want to look into the other room. She could feel her mother's eyes on her. That wasn't the real problem. What did she say to this man she'd fallen into bed with, and later learned it was all a lie? She couldn't make idle conversation. "If that's lunch, my mother and her friends are in the other room."

"I better get it to them then. Will you be staying?"

She shook her head, wishing she could get her heart rate under control. "No, I have a lot of errands to run. In fact I should be going right now. Bye, Noah."

He frowned. "I'll be seeing you around, Lilly."

Like the chicken she was, she practically ran out the door. Why did he have to come back to town? And why did he have to talk about babies?

She straightened, then started down the street. She wasn't lying about errands. It was nearly one o'clock and she had an hour before her meeting with Mark Greenberg. He'd been Mike's lawyer for the business, and he also served as his divorce lawyer. She was thinking positively, hoping that Mike left a little something for Robbie and Kasey. At least they'd have something of their father's things since he wouldn't be around for them.

Lilly's thoughts returned to Noah. In the weeks he'd been in town, he'd spent more time with the kids than their own father had. The hours he'd spent with her had her dreaming again, dreaming of happily ever after.

How quickly things change.

Coop watched out the window as Lilly headed down the street. He had to hold himself back from chasing after her. He didn't have the right to anyway. He was trying to give her time, but he wasn't a patient man. Not when it came to Lilly. That was the reason when he returned yesterday he'd talked with Beth first, trying to clear up some of his deceptions. Why he couldn't tell anyone who he was, or anything about his job.

He was encouraged that Beth Staley understood his dilemma. She also loved her daughter and didn't want to see her get hurt again. It had taken some talking to convince Beth that he cared about Lilly and the kids. Beth had believed him.

Now if he could only convince Lilly.

Coop went outside onto Main Street and his gaze went across to the Dark Moon Arcade. He and the sheriff had tried to find all the local drug connections in town, but things were a little sketchy on that place. Coop had a feeling. What was the draw to this hangout? Whatever it was, they weren't going to get any help from Santos. He'd already asked for a lawyer.

Coop knew that if he walked into the arcade in his Ranger's uniform, the bad guys would scatter in all directions. Finding all the drug pushers was wishful thinking, but he wanted to clean up Kerry Springs. Right now it looked like a long shot, but he hoped to have a future here.

"Coop, how long are you going to be up there?" Robbie called as he looked up from below.

With his paintbrush in hand, Coop leaned down from the ladder to see the boy with his baseball glove on. "Well, I'd say maybe a few hours. I want to finish this trim for your grandma."

"A few hours," the child groaned. "It'll be dark and I'll hafta to go to bed. Man, I'll never get to play catch."

Coop hated to disappoint the boy, but he'd promised Beth he'd finish the windows. He owed her for the use of the cottage over his four-week stay. He was also going to continue to work at Vista Verde while he was off duty, waiting for his transfer from El Paso to the Ranger company in San Antonio. Although he had plenty of vacation time saved up, he wanted to stay in town permanently. And hopefully, he'd be hanging around long enough to have time for Lilly to trust him. That meant he needed to be honest with her.

"I guess it couldn't hurt to take a short break."

That brought a smile to Robbie's face as Coop carried his bucket and brush down the ladder. "Yeah, it's sure hot up there."

"Yeah, too hot to paint, but not to play baseball, huh, Coop?"

"It's never too hot for baseball." He placed his brush and bucket in the shade, and covered the brush with plastic. "You got my glove?"

"Yep, here it is." Robbie handed it to him. "I haven't been practicing 'cause nobody wanted to play with me."

"I know your mom and grandma are busy." He tossed Robbie the ball and the boy missed it. "That's okay, try again. Remember keep your eye on the ball."

Coop tossed it again and this time, the boy caught it.

"So why couldn't Kasey toss a ball with you?"

"She has a new friend. Lindsey," he mimicked in a whiny voice. "Kasey's gonna get in trouble again."

Coop didn't like the sound of that. "Why do you say that?"

The boy looked away with a shrug.

"Robbie, if Kasey is doing something she shouldn't, she could be in more trouble than just with her mother."

Robbie paused for a long time. "I promised her I wouldn't tell." He shook his head. "I can't break a promise."

Coop went to the child and squatted down in front of him. "Could your sister get hurt?"

The six-year-old's eyes rounded. "She's doing it so Lindsey won't get hurt."

Coop tried to remain calm. "Rob, you know I'm a Texas Ranger and it's my job to protect the people in this state. If Kasey and Lindsey are in trouble, I've got to help them. So where did she go?"

"The arcade to find Lindsey 'cause that's where Lindsey's boyfriend goes."

Damn, he was afraid of that. They were thirteen-year-old girls and he knew for a fact that there weren't any nice teenage boys who hung out at the Dark Moon. "Okay, Rob, you did good. Now, get in my truck and we'll go get the girls."

"Just don't let Kasey be mad at me," he said, fighting tears. Then the boy took off.

At the cottage, Coop grabbed a clean shirt, badge and sidearm then hurried to his truck. He backed out of the driveway and thought about calling for backup, but so far there wasn't cause to have the sheriff come storming in.

He sent up a prayer that it stayed that way.

Two hours later, Lilly was in a daze as she came out of the lawyer's office. Then it turned to excitement as the details of the meeting really sunk in. She was in shock to discover that Mike's death was now ruled a murder instead of a suicide, so his life insurance policy would pay out. There would be money for college for the kids, to help them find another home.

The biggest shock was that Perry Landscaping belonged to Robbie and Kasey, too. Although Stephanie had laid claim to the business, she'd forced Mike to sign the business over to her.

Mr. Greenberg assured Lilly that whatever papers Stephanie had proving any ownership of the company weren't legal. Perry Landscaping belonged to the children, and Lilly was to act on their behalf until they became of age.

She had a lot to think about. First was to stop by the Blind Stitch and tell her mother the news. Then she saw the patrol car at the arcade across the street. She frowned, seeing the familiar truck. It was Noah's. Was he doing an investigation? Then a small figure in the front seat caught her attention. Robbie?

Glancing in both directions, she crossed the street onto the sidewalk and hurried up next to the cab. "Robbie, what are you doing here?"

"Oh, hi, Mom. I had to come with Coop 'cause he didn't want to leave me home by myself."

"Alone? You weren't alone. Your sister was watching you." A feeling of dread washed over her. "Where's Noah?"

He pointed toward the arcade. "Inside there."

She swallowed hard against her panic. "Where's Kasey?"

"She's inside, too. Don't worry, Mom, Coop's helping her. He wore his gun and everything."

Lilly turned to see another patrol car with its lights flashing as it pulled up and two deputies got out and rushed inside. She opened the truck door and pulled her son out. "Robbie, I want you to go to the Blind Stitch and stay with your grandmother."

Robbie frowned. "Ah, Mom, but I want to stay here. Coop is going to arrest the bad guys."

She ignored his request and helped her son out of the truck. After checking traffic she watched Robbie run across and into the store. She headed to the arcade, but wasn't surprised to see a deputy guarding the door. Too bad, she wasn't about to let anyone stop her from getting to her child.

Coop could breathe easier now that the three suspects were cuffed and the sheriff had arrived to read them their Miranda rights. He'd been lucky to walk in during the middle of a drug transaction and catch them by surprise. That didn't happen often, like never.

Kasey and her friend Lindsey weren't anywhere near the drugs, or the struggle. But it was still too close. Lindsey's so-called friends were dealers, barely out of their teens themselves, but the arcade was to be their new turf.

Once the DEA agents arrived with a warrant, they began to search the premises and found a dummy wall in the back room. It housed enough illegal drugs to get the arcade owner, scumbag Tony Lazar, more than a fine and a slap on the wrist. They lucked out with the arcade's main supplier Santos being shut down. Lazar had to scramble to keep his clientele in drugs, so he was working with these punks.

The sheriff came up to him. "Did you get a tip?"

"Yeah, from a six-year-old, telling me his sister was here."

Bradshaw shook his head. "Hopefully Lazar won't get off and we'll finally be able to shut this place down." Smiling, the sheriff held out his hand. "It's been nice working with you, Ranger Cooper."

"I'm only glad that everything turned out well. We both know it doesn't always happen that way." He nodded to the two frightened looking girls huddled together. "Do you know Lindsey's parents?"

Brad nodded. "I gave them a call, but I'm taking her home."

Once Lindsey left with the sheriff, Coop went over to Kasey. "You okay?"

She shook her head. "I think I'm gonna get sick."

He led her over to a chair and sat her down. "Take some deep breaths."

Kasey did as she was told. After a few minutes she looked better.

"You okay now?"

"Yes. Oh, Coop, Mom's going to go ballistic. I'll be grounded for the rest of my life."

"You don't feel you deserve some punishment? You left your brother, too."

She looked sad. "Coop, I knew you would be there."

He frowned. "Still, what you did was dangerous, Kasey. Those guys were dealing drugs. Not exactly the best environment for a barely thirteen-year-old girl."

"I didn't do it for me. I was trying to talk Lindsey out of meeting these guys."

Coop shook his head. "No, good judgment would have been to get an adult to help you. Did you see the weapons I took off those boys?"

She nodded as a tear ran down her cheek. "I'm sorry, Coop. I was so scared." She broke down and he pulled her into an embrace as if it was the most natural thing in the world to do. She was so little, so vulnerable. "You scared me, too, Kasey. I care about you, your brother and your mom. How could I go back to her and tell her something happened to her little girl?" Emotions nearly choked him. "It would break her heart."

"Coop's right."

They both jerked around to see Lilly. Kasey jumped up and hurried to her and the crying began once again. "I'm so sorry, Mom."

Coop moved away, giving mother and daughter some privacy. As much as he wanted to be a part of the reunion, he had no right to be there. Not yet anyway.

It was after nine o'clock that night when Lilly left Kasey's bedroom. She'd taken the time to listen to how frightened her daughter had been when she and Lindsey got caught in the middle of an argument over drug turf.

If Noah hadn't been there...

Lilly shivered as she brushed the hair back from her sleeping daughter's face. She didn't want to think about that. Only that he had been there today.

Once again Noah Cooper had come to the rescue. And that was what she needed to do, too. To be there for her kids. This past year she'd been so angry over what had happened to her, she'd forgotten about the two most important people, her kids. No more.

After she kissed Kasey good-night, she walked down to the kitchen and found her mother and Sean in a tight embrace, sharing those soft intimate words that lovers share. Envy struck her. She brushed it aside and started to back out, then they noticed her.

"Lilly, please, don't leave," her mother called. "We want to talk to you."

She returned and sat down at the table across from the couple.

"First of all, how are you doing, lass?" Sean asked, his big hands reaching out and engulfing hers.

"I'm fine, just worried about Kasey. I think some counseling would help her. And since she's going to be grounded until next month, at least I won't have to worry about her." She tried to make light of it. "I should have tried harder to get through to her."

"No, you're doing your job," her mother said. "Kasey is old enough to know right from wrong. She used poor judgment. Just like Coop said."

Sean raised his eyes heavenward. "Praise be for Noah."

"And I can never thank him enough."

"There's something else I need to tell you, Lilly," her mother began. "Coop has moved back here…temporarily. That's the reason he knew that Kasey had gone to the arcade. He's staying in the cottage for the next month."

He wasn't leaving town? Right, he had to do follow-up on the Santos case.

"If it upsets you…he can make other arrangements."

She felt all kinds of mixed emotions, excitement one of them. She pushed it aside. "You have every right to rent the cottage to him, Mom." She suddenly felt exhausted. "I'm tired. I think I'll go up to bed, too."

Beth got up and went to her daughter. She hugged her. "A long night's sleep will do you good. It's been a heck of a day."

Trying to hold it together, Lilly nodded, unable to speak. She wanted nothing more than to bury herself under the covers and sleep for a long time.

"I think you know that a man like Noah Cooper doesn't show up on your doorstep every day." Beth looked at Sean. "So when he comes calling—for a second time—don't turn him away."

Lilly smiled at the couple, knowing how long it took for both of them to find one another. Their happiness was wonderful to see, but also painful. Not everyone was so lucky.

What if she couldn't be the woman that Noah needed? She already knew that she still wasn't the woman she needed to be.

CHAPTER FOURTEEN

Hours later, Coop pulled into his parking spot at the Staley house. He'd been at the sheriff's department with DEA, and then his captain, for hours. He finally begged off and said he needed to get some sleep. After all, this was supposed to be his vacation. He'd worked so long to find Delgado that he hadn't taken any time off. He planned to use every minute of his time here to woo Lilly. Did they even use that term any longer? And did he even know how to do it right? Since he'd avoided all relationships for years, he wasn't sure how to begin.

Climbing out of the truck, he locked it and headed to his front door. He'd think about it tomorrow. Maybe he'd ask advice from Alex or Sean. Both men seemed to know how to keep a woman happy. He'd take any pointers on how to win Lilly.

Maybe it was a crazy idea. Could a thirty-seven-year-old man suddenly change and take a chance at having a family?

Coop started to put the key in the lock and discovered the door was ajar. A warning went off. He placed a hand on the weapon at his waist, ready if this was retaliation for earlier. Pushing on the door revealed a dim light and he spotted a shadowy figure seated on the sofa.

He blinked and took another look. Lilly?

He released his weapon and walked in. She turned toward him and tried to smile, but he could see she looked a little tired.

"Lilly, is something wrong?"

She stood and crossed the room. "No, and I'm sorry for the intrusion. I guess I got too comfortable in the quiet. Anyway I wanted to thank you for what you did for Kasey today."

He didn't want her gratitude. "There's no reason to thank me," he told her. "You have to know I would never let anything happen to Kasey or Robbie."

She nodded. "I still wanted to tell you how grateful I am that you were there for Kasey. She and I had a long talk tonight, and I'm going to get her some help, some counseling." She glanced away and drew a shaky breath. "I've been so worried about me that I'd forgotten how all this affected the kids. And they are so vulnerable…"

He couldn't stand to see her fight so hard to hold it together. He reached for her pulling her into his arms, locking her in an embrace, not wanting her to ever leave. His chest tightened as he felt her warm tears against his shirt, and wished he could take away all her pain and sadness. "It's going to be okay, Lilly," he breathed against her ear.

She raised her head and looked at him in the dim light. "How can you say that?"

"Because I know you. I know your strength, your determination. Kasey and Robbie know they can depend on you."

A tear hit her cheek. "I don't think I'm exactly a candidate for mother of the year."

"You're a great mother." When she didn't look convinced, he went on. "I should know bad mothers. My own didn't have time for me or my brother. She was too busy trying to find the next guy who would take care of her." His gaze locked on hers. "You're strong and loving, Lilly."

He cupped her face and held his breath waiting for her to pull away. She didn't. "Don't ever think you're not." He brushed a kiss across her lips, her sweet lips.

She sucked in a breath. "Noah…"

He didn't give her a chance to say any more. Like a starved man he went back for more. This time he needed to let her know how much he cared about her, desired her, but more than that, he wanted to be a part of her life.

He pulled her against him as his mouth moved over hers. When his tongue touched her lips, she opened for him so he could deepen the kiss. He eagerly tasted her sweetness, aching for more. He wanted all of her.

Finally he tore his mouth away, wanting to tell her how he felt about her. "Lilly, I've missed you so much."

She tensed and pulled free. "I'm sorry." She shook her head. "I didn't plan for this to happen. Thank you again for what you did."

He let her go. "I care about you, Lilly."

She turned away. "I can't do this now, Noah. The kids need me…"

He knew she'd gone through so much. "Let me help you."

"I have to do this on my own." She turned to face him. "Besides, you'll be gone soon on another case."

He couldn't make her any promises, yet. "What if I'm here, Lilly?"

She stood there unable to speak, but he saw the anguish on her face. "I need to go," she said, her voice rough with emotion. She walked out, closing the door behind her, leaving Coop alone. He'd been alone most of his life, but this time, he wasn't going to let her walk away. "No, Lilly, I can't give up on us."

* * *

Over the next few days, work had been the only thing that kept Coop distracted from Lilly. Not seeing or hearing from her, he was beginning to doubt that they were going to come together.

He cut another piece of crown molding.

"Hey, Coop, you're playing havoc with the overtime."

Hearing Alex Casali, he turned around. "I thought you wanted the model home ready to show by the weekend?"

"I do, but I don't want you working so many hours that you get injured. Don't you have a pretty lady to spend time with?"

He wished. "She's spending time with her kids. She needs some time. Oh, hell, truth is, I could be wasting my time."

Alex nodded and pushed his hard hat back off his forehead. "Yeah, it's hard to know what they want."

"Alessandro Casali, you didn't just say that."

They both swung around to see Allison Casali. The pretty auburn-haired woman was visibly angry. "Coop, ignore this man. If you care about Lilly then you figure out what she needs from you."

"I do care for her. But she keeps pushing me away."

"Then push back. Let Lilly know you aren't going to hurt her like Mike did." She raised her hand. "To be honest, their marriage was in trouble long before Santos showed up. That did a lot of damage to Lilly. Trust comes hard." Allison glanced at her husband. "It's all about sharing things."

Alex pulled his wife against his side. "Yeah, that one was a hard one for me." He grinned down at Allison. "But the rewards are so worth it."

"How do I convince Lilly?" Coop asked, envious of the exchange between the two.

"Prove to her that you're going to be there no matter what. That you love her."

"Tell her?"

Allison shook her head. "No, show her."

Lilly awoke Saturday morning feeling a little groggy. Lack of sleep will do that to a person, especially when it's several days. She sat up in bed and saw the reason: Mike's letter. It took her a while to be brave enough to read, then finally, two days ago, she'd realized that if she was going to move ahead with her life, her kids' lives, she needed to deal with the past.

Mike's handwritten letter had explained so many things. The reason why he'd left his family. The reason he'd divorced her and refused to see the kids. He told her how much he loved her and the kids, and he'd wished he'd spent more time with them.

Lilly had allowed herself the tears for what they'd lost. Mike had done a wonderful thing for his family and she'd always love him for that. But she couldn't go back to that time.

Yesterday, Lilly had shared parts of the letter with Kasey and Robbie and she held them as they all shed tears. It had been the first time that either one of them let go and showed emotions over their father's death.

Later, she'd taken them both to the cemetery to see Mike's grave again. She wanted to do everything possible to help them heal. In time they'd all deal with the sadness, hers included.

Robbie announced that his dad was a hero. And Kasey's change in attitude was remarkable. She'd always been so close to her father; Lilly still had no idea how much his death had affected her. Maybe because she'd been too wrapped up in her own bitterness to see her daughter's pain.

While the kids headed back to the car, Lilly had stayed at the graveside and made her own peace with Mike. The man she'd been married to for thirteen years. The man she'd loved since college. She knew they'd been having problems a long time before their breakup. They'd been going in different directions for a few years before he'd left her. Their busy careers had a lot to do with it. But they'd both been to blame for the failures. No matter what, she would always love the father of her children. She would never let Kasey and Robbie forget the man who'd died protecting them.

She wiped away the tears. It was time, and she finally said goodbye to her past.

Smiling, Lilly sat up and hugged her knees. She began to think about her future and a certain Texas Ranger who'd been haunting her day and night. Did he have room in his life for her and her kids? Was there a chance for them?

Whoa, she needed to slow down. Since she hadn't seen him at all in the past few days, she wondered if he'd given up on them and left.

"He'd better not." She jumped into the shower and dressed in record time. It was time she talked to the kids about Noah Cooper.

She went downstairs for breakfast, hearing the happy chatter and laughter in the kitchen. At the stove was Kasey making pancakes and Robbie was seated at the counter, telling one of his silly jokes. Her mother was seated at the table, supervising.

Robbie spotted her. "Mom, you waked up."

"Yes, I did." She smiled. "Looks like you've all been busy this morning."

"Yeah, we're happy today," Robbie said.

She knew it had a lot to do with the closure they were all feeling. She had her kids back.

"And I get to go see where Coop works and—"

"Robbie," his grandmother said in a warning tone.

Her son looked back at her. "If you say it's okay," he began again. "Oh, please, Mom. Please! We want to go to where Coop works. You're invited, too."

That would be wonderful, if only… "Honey, Noah works in El Paso."

Robbie shook his head. "No, Mom, Coop's other work, building houses for Mr. C."

Lilly shot a look at her mother. "He's still working on Vista Verde?"

Beth Staley didn't even look ashamed that she'd left that part out of any conversation they'd had in the past.

"Yep, he sure is," Kasey answered. "And they're having a picnic today for all the employees' families." Her daughter smiled as she brought a stack of pancakes to the table. "Maybe he might even buy one of the houses."

"That would be cool!" Robbie got up on his knees, stabbed the cake on top and dropped it on his plate. "Then Coop can be around to play baseball with me. So can we go? There's swimming in the new pool at the park there, too."

Lilly sent a curious glance at her mother. "What are they talking about?"

The older woman shrugged. "Well, if a man wants to settle down, it seems natural to find a house. I mean the cottage is a little small."

Her head was spinning. "But he lives and works in El Paso."

"I'm only saying, 'Where there's a will, there's a way,'" Beth Staley said.

Lilly's heart pounded in her chest. Noah Cooper living

in Kerry Springs? Permanently? She tried to calm herself. "Well, he hasn't said anything to me about it."

Her mother frowned. "If you gave the guy a chance, maybe he would."

An hour later, Lilly arrived at the construction site with two excited kids. Their mother wasn't exactly calm, either. After last week, and the kiss they'd shared at the cottage, she'd been chicken. So she'd stayed clear of Noah Cooper. Yet, she couldn't stay away today, and she found she was excited that he was possibly staying in town.

She pulled up in front of the trailer and parked next to Allison Casali's SUV. There was also a sign hanging from a 4x4 post that read, Verde Vista Family Picnic.

"See, Mom, everyone is invited today." Robbie turned to her with a smile. "Kasey and me are part of Coop's family for the day."

Lilly nodded as she climbed out of the car. There were several other families with their kids headed toward the end of the street to the community park where the pool was located.

"Mom, can I go find Coop?"

"We'll all go together," she told her son, not sure what was really going on. But she was going to find out.

Allison Casali and her older daughter, Cherry, came out of the construction trailer. The ten-year-old had on shorts and a sleeveless top.

Lilly smiled and waved. "Hello, Allison. Hi, Cherry."

"Hi, Mrs. P. Hi, Robbie, Kasey." The auburn-haired girl handed them baseball caps with the company logo on them. "You're here with Coop?"

"Yep." The boy puffed out his chest. "He's going to be my dad for today."

"And mine, too," Kasey answered.

Lilly didn't know how to correct them, yet she found she didn't want to, either.

Cherry said, "Come inside and I'll get your tickets for the games and the swimming passes."

The kids disappeared into the trailer and Allison stayed with Lilly. "I think it's nice that Coop is so involved with your kids."

"I just don't want them to get hurt…if things don't work out."

Allison frowned. "I know a lot has happened, Lilly, I've been there, too. If this thing between you and Coop is meant to be, it'll work out. That is if you want it to."

Lilly looked at the woman who seemed to have it all. Allison got a second chance herself, along with her daughter when she met Alex Casali. "I know things worked out for you and Alex. Of course I would like to find happiness like that."

Allison arched an eyebrow. "You think it was easy getting that stubborn man to admit to his feelings?" She pointed toward the trailer. "No way. But I knew what I wanted and I fought for Alex, Lilly. Not saying I wasn't scared to death, and I nearly walked away from him more than once." A bright smile appeared on Allison's face. "But when he said the words, 'I love you,' I was his." Allison sobered. "Ask yourself, do you want to hear Coop say the words?"

As frightened as she was, she managed to nod.

Just then the kids came out of the trailer and Robbie spotted Noah. "Coop!" Her son took off toward him and Noah hugged the boy. Kasey was next.

"What's not to love about that man?" Allison sighed. "Kids and animals are a great judge of character. I'd say your Noah Cooper wins hands down. Your kids are sure he's a winner. Go for it, Lilly. You deserve to have some happiness." Then Allison walked inside the trailer.

Lilly only had time to put on a smile as Noah arrived with her kids hanging all over him.

Those dark eyes locked on her. "Hi, Lilly."

"Hi, Noah."

Coop couldn't take his eyes off this woman; he was hungry for her. She was dressed in white shorts and a pretty blue sleeveless blouse, with her glorious brunette hair lying in curls around her shoulders. He just wanted to keep looking at her. He'd missed her so much.

His hope was they'd be spending a lot more time together in the future. That was if he could do this right.

"Well, I should go," Lilly said, interrupting his thoughts. "What time do you want me back to pick them up?"

"No, don't," he coaxed, a little too anxious. "I invited you, too. Besides, I need your advice."

She seemed reluctant as he took her hand. "Come on, I want to show you all something before we go to the picnic. You, too, kids," he added and they started toward the model homes.

Since it was Saturday, and with the families on the site, the work was at a standstill. He waved to some of the other employees as they headed toward the park that had been designed for the home owners. It included a community pool, a clubhouse, several playgrounds and a baseball diamond.

"The park is a nice addition," Lilly said.

"It is. Alex and Allison wanted a place close where kids could play and parents didn't have to worry. Perry's did all the landscaping." He smiled at her, knowing she'd manage the company until this project was completed.

She nodded toward the young trees lining the parkways and the green lawns already taking root in the yards of the completed model home. "Mike would be proud of the work."

All Coop did was nod as he took the family down the sidewalk passing two different houses.

"Thought you might like to see what I've been working on."

"Are you sure it's okay?"

He smiled. "I'm sure. Allison has already selected the furniture and it's staged for viewing tomorrow." He tugged on her hand and they took the walkway to an inviting porch and double mahogany doors of the two-story house.

"Oh, my, this is so different than I'd expected. It's so large!"

Inside the entry there were high coved ceilings. A formal dining room was off to one side, on the other side an office. What drew their attention was the open staircase leading upstairs. The kids took off for the second floor.

"And all the trim details." She ran her fingers over the recently stained wainscoting."

"So you like it?"

"Oh, yes."

He smiled. "That's my work."

"I'm impressed."

"Then come on, I want you to see this." He reached for her hand again and led her through a hall and into the open kitchen. Three walls were lined with cherry cabinets and granite countertops. The appliances were stainless steel and there was a big island, too.

She seemed speechless.

Coop watched Lilly's gaze moved around, then to the attached family room. "There's a fireplace," he added. "And of course a place for a flat screen television. A major necessity these days." He grinned, hearing the kids upstairs.

"I should get them down here," Lilly said.

"We'll go up instead."

They climbed the stairs to the spacious second level. "I like all the openness," she commented.

Enough to live here? Coop thought.

Lilly peeked into a small bedroom, then another looking for her children.

Robbie came out into the hall. "I want this bedroom, Mom."

"And I want this one," Kasey called from farther away.

Lilly blushed. "Kids, we're not living here."

Kasey then came out of one of the rooms. "Mom, you're not going to believe it, there are four bedrooms, and this master suite has a closet to die for. And a huge bathroom with a whirlpool tub. The other bedrooms are big, too."

Noah had to intervene. "Kasey, why don't you take your brother downstairs and look at the kitchen and family room?"

"Okay, come on, Robbie," the teenager said hiding a smile.

Once they were gone, Noah took Lilly into the master suite. He wanted her to love everything. Beyond the entrance was a small sitting room with a love seat, a chair and a side tables decorating the area. They continued on to the main room where a huge four-poster bed was the centerpiece, illuminated by light from a row of windows.

"Oh, my, this place just gets better and better. Allison did a wonderful job with the furniture."

Lilly let out a gasp as she walked up to the bed. She reached out a shaky hand and touched the quilt draped across the end of the mattress.

She finally glanced at him. "My mother's quilting group were working on this a few weeks ago. How did it get here?"

"Beth gave it to me."

She only stared at him with those glistening green eyes. "Why?"

"I wanted something personal. Something that would make it feel like home to you. If not this model, there are three others we can look at.

She blinked in surprise.

That was his cue. "Lilly, since I've met you, it seems like all I've done is mess everything up." He stepped back, taking a big breath. "You were right. I had no business getting involved personally, but I'd lost all objectivity when it came you. I'm sorry, I know I hurt you. That was never my intention." His gaze remained on hers. "I'm asking you for another chance, Lilly. I hope I can convince you I'm worthy of your trust."

"Oh, Noah."

He ignored her plea. "I'm moving to Kerry Springs permanently. I've already got the transfer to work out of San Antonio. No more undercover. I want to come home to you and the kids. To make a life with you."

Tears filled her eyes.

"Okay, I understand if you need some time. I'll give you time, but let me tell you one thing, Lilly Perry, there's no one who could love you as much as I do. All I ask is that you give me a chance to prove to you that I can be the man you need. I won't let you down."

Lilly put her fingers on her trembling lips, having trouble believe this. "You love me?"

He looked in her eyes and nodded. "Until I think I'll go crazy if I can't be a part of your life. I never thought I'd want all this, a home, hearth and kids. Then you came along. When I was working on your mother's house, all I was hoping for was for you to come outside. I wanted to see you, talk with you. I had no right to touch you, to kiss you. And that incredible night we spent together making love." He moved closer. "God, no, Lilly, you were never, I repeat never, part of my job. You were pure pleasure."

"Oh, Noah. I know that now. It took me some time, but I realized I wanted to be with you, too."

He cupped her face with his hands and his mouth closed over hers in a gentle kiss.

Lilly didn't want to fight it any longer. She wanted this man. No more fears; she was going after what she wanted and all that Noah Cooper was offering her.

She tore her mouth away. "Oh, Noah, I love you so much."

A big grin appeared and he lifted her up and swung her around, letting out a shout, making her laugh.

He set her down. "Oh, darlin', you'll never regret it, I promise."

"I'm sorry it took me so long to sort out my feelings. But hearing what Mike had done for us, it threw me. The kids, too. I also needed to say goodbye to the past before I could come to you."

He sobered. "I hope you mean it because I want nothing short of you being my wife. I want to marry you, Lilly Perry. Maybe not next week." He searched her face. "Take all the time you need, well, not too much time."

Lilly shook her head. "The only thing I need to hear is that you love me. I don't need to sort out anything else, Noah Cooper." She slipped her arms around his waist. "And I want to share it with you and the kids. So yes, I'll marry you."

He started to kiss her again and she gasped, "There might be one more thing."

"Anything," he breathed.

"You're too easy, Mr. Texas Ranger. Just so you know, I'm going to require more than half of that big closet." She smiled, feeling light-headed. "Do you think we could negotiate something?"

He grinned. "We definitely can work that out." He pulled her close and his mouth closed over hers. Soon they were lost in each other.

They barely noticed when the door opened and two kids poked their heads in. "Looks like we better pick out bedrooms after all," Kasey said.

Robbie added with a grin, "And we get a new dad, too. This is the best day ever." The kids took off down the stairs.

Coop broke off the kiss and smiled down at Lilly. "This is going to be the best life ever."

EPILOGUE

THE summer ended and school had been back in session for over a month. Lilly couldn't believe time had flown by so fast. Yet, it still wasn't fast enough.

Although she'd wanted to wait a few months before Noah became her husband, she was quickly regretting that choice.

When they first set the wedding date, she had wanted to get things in order. To have a clean slate to start her life with Noah. That meant the landscaping business had to be sold. Too many bad memories for both her and the kids. The foreman, Jace Rankin, had been eager to buy the company. Lilly felt good that none of the employees would lose their jobs.

Part of the money from the sale was invested for the kids. Another part, she invested in their new family home. She wanted to be a full partner in her marriage to Noah. Never again did she want to be left out of any part of the decision making, the good or the bad. Even though Noah wanted to be the breadwinner for his family, he understood.

Noah also had made changes. He worked out of the Ranger company in San Antonio, then returned home to Kerry Springs at night. There still would be times when he worked on cases that he couldn't be there, but no undercover work.

Then she and the kids went into counseling. They'd worked through issues with Mike. Noah even joined in some sessions to help as a family. She was blessed that her future husband loved her children as much as they loved him.

Lilly smiled at her man as he walked through her mother's front door. He wore a dark suit in honor of the special day. She felt a warm shiver rush down her spine seeing how handsome he looked. He turned on a smile and she nearly melted on the spot. What was not to love?

"Hello, beautiful." He kissed her sweetly.

Lilly glanced down at her blush-colored dress. The bodice was fitted to the waist and the skirt had several layers of sheer fabric. "Thought I'd dress up," she said. "After all, it is my mother's wedding day."

"I wish it were ours."

Lilly felt the same way, too. "Sorry I made you wait."

He placed a finger against her lips. "You're worth the wait. But I'm still counting the hours until you're mine."

She was a lucky woman. Noah had cut his vacation short so they could take a honeymoon later. All she knew about it was they would be headed to an island somewhere they could be alone and concentrate on only the two of them. Even Millie offered to stay at the house and watch the kids. All the ladies of the Quilter's Corner were taking turns helping.

"I only need you, Noah Cooper."

He started to say something when someone called to her. "Sorry, I've got to help with this."

"How about we meet at the cottage later?"

She agreed, then gave him a quick kiss. She took off, gathered the kids and went to help her mother with finishing touches. For a small backyard wedding, there was a lot to do. Lilly was happy that her mother had found a life with Sean. After their honeymoon to Ireland, the couple would come back to Kerry Springs and start up the new business of selling Rafferty's Barbecue Sauce.

With guests seated out in the yard and the music playing softly, Beth Staley made her way down to the kitchen. She was wearing an ivory sheath-style dress. Her hair was adorned with some baby's breath, and she held a bouquet of colorful roses. She looked so lovely.

Lilly hugged her. "You're a vision, Mom. I'm so happy for you and Sean."

"Thank you, Lilly." She blotted at her tears. "We're both so lucky, aren't we? To find such wonderful men."

Lilly nodded, knowing that no matter the circumstances of meeting Noah, he'd turned out to be the love of her life.

The sound of music filled the room. "Ready?"

"Oh, yes." Beth Staley beamed as she took her daughter's arm and together they walked out onto the porch and down the steps. Wedding guests sat on either side of the aisle of green grass. Under an arch of flowers at the edge of the yard stood the handsome groom, Sean, with his two sons, Evan and Matt, standing beside him. He smiled at seeing his bride. They approached and Sean kissed Lilly's cheek, then took Beth's hand. Lilly went to stand beside Noah and Kasey and Robbie. Noah's hand engulfed hers as she looked around the yard, filled with family and friends.

She caught Noah's gaze on hers as the minister announced, "You may kiss your bride."

Noah leaned down and placed his mouth on hers, pushing out the rest of the world.

Hours later, Noah arranged it so they had the evening to themselves. Something that he'd missed the last few weeks with all the wedding plans, and finishing the house to make sure it was ready for the family to move in. But tonight, with the newlyweds headed for Ireland, and the kids tucked into bed in the house, that meant Lilly was his for a few hours. He didn't plan to waste a second of their time.

At the cottage, he opened wine and poured some into glasses, then lit candles. Stolen hours were all they had now, but in another month, he wouldn't have to leave her… ever.

"Noah." The door opened and Lilly walked inside. "I got your note."

He walked over to greet her. Like he'd done, she'd changed into jeans after the wedding guests left.

He took her in his arms and kissed her. He needed her more than he ever thought possible. Her smile, her touch. "I love you."

"I love you, too." She smiled up at him. "Are you going to kidnap me tonight?"

"Is that your fantasy? I do have a pair of handcuffs in the other room."

She shook her head. "You don't need them, Mr. Texas Ranger. I'll come willingly."

He kissed her again. "I wish we were already married."

"I know." She smiled again. "Look at it this way, I'm giving you a chance to back out. I mean, you're taking on a teenage girl and an active six-year-old. No privacy."

"Sorry, lady, you're stuck with me for a long time."

She wrapped her arms around his neck. "I'm not going anywhere, either."

Coop leaned down and kissed her. It started out slow and easy, but quickly it turned hungry…fast. Their few stolen moments the past few months hadn't been enough.

He broke off the kiss. "I want you, Lilly," he said. "But I want to talk to you about something first."

She smiled. "I thought you had something else in mind besides talking."

"Give me a few minutes and we'll get back to it."

Lilly sobered and released him. "Okay. Is there a problem?"

"Not in the way you think." He backed away a little. "You know I care about the kids."

She nodded. "Yes, and they feel the same way about you."

"How would you be with me adopting Kasey and Rob?" He raised a hand. "I know they were close to their father, but I want them to feel part of us. I was a stepchild, and I hated it. I want your kids to know that I love them. For us to be a real family."

Lilly blinked back tears. "Oh, Noah. I don't think I could love you more than I do right now. I'm sure Kasey and Robbie would love the idea, too. I just don't want you to feel pressured about doing this."

He drew her back into his arms. "Are you kidding? Besides getting the woman of my dreams, I get a bonus with two great kids."

She slipped her arms around his neck and kissed him. Not a sweet peck but a blow your socks off kiss. When they broke away, Coop said, "I take it you think I'll make a good parent."

She nodded. "You're going to be the best, but I think maybe you need some practice with infants."

Noah nearly choked as his throat dried up. "A baby? You want a baby? I never thought…"

"I know we haven't talked about it." Her gaze locked on his. "I'll understand if you don't want another child."

His chest tightened. "Oh, God, Lilly. A baby. Our baby." He pulled her back into his arms. "When I saw you holding little Mick…I had dreams about you carrying my child."

He placed his hand against her flat stomach. "Yes, yes, I want our baby more than anything."

She beamed. "So do I, but maybe not right away."

"As much time as you need. I love you so much."

She went back into his arms and brushed her mouth over his. Noah knew that his life was going to change, but only for the better. It might not be perfect all the time, but with his new family, it would come pretty damn close.

* * * * *

Coming Next Month

Available November 8, 2011

#4273 SNOWBOUND WITH HER HERO
Rebecca Winters

#4274 THE PLAYBOY'S GIFT
Teresa Carpenter

#4275 FIREFIGHTER UNDER THE MISTLETOE
Melissa McClone

#4276 BLIND DATE RIVALS
Nina Harrington

#4277 THE PRINCESS NEXT DOOR
Jackie Braun

#4278 RODEO DADDY
Rugged Ranchers
Soraya Lane

You can find more information on upcoming
Harlequin® titles, free excerpts and more at
www.HarlequinInsideRomance.com.

REQUEST YOUR FREE BOOKS!
2 FREE NOVELS PLUS 2 FREE GIFTS!

Harlequin *Romance*

From the Heart, For the Heart

YES! Please send me 2 FREE Harlequin® Romance novels and my 2 FREE gifts (gifts are worth about $10). After receiving them, if I don't wish to receive any more books, I can return the shipping statement marked "cancel". If I don't cancel, I will receive 6 brand-new novels every month and be billed just $4.09 per book in the U.S. or $4.49 per book in Canada. That's a savings of at least 14% off the cover price! It's quite a bargain! Shipping and handling is just 50¢ per book in the U.S. and 75¢ per book in Canada.* I understand that accepting the 2 free books and gifts places me under no obligation to buy anything. I can always return a shipment and cancel at any time. Even if I never buy another book, the two free books and gifts are mine to keep forever.

116/316 HDN FESE

Name	(PLEASE PRINT)	
Address		Apt. #
City	State/Prov.	Zip/Postal Code
Signature (if under 18, a parent or guardian must sign)		

Mail to the **Reader Service:**
IN U.S.A.: P.O. Box 1867, Buffalo, NY 14240-1867
IN CANADA: P.O. Box 609, Fort Erie, Ontario L2A 5X3

Not valid for current subscribers to Harlequin Romance books.

**Are you a subscriber to Harlequin Romance books
and want to receive the larger-print edition?
Call 1-800-873-8635 or visit www.ReaderService.com.**

* Terms and prices subject to change without notice. Prices do not include applicable taxes. Sales tax applicable in N.Y. Canadian residents will be charged applicable taxes. Offer not valid in Quebec. This offer is limited to one order per household. All orders subject to credit approval. Credit or debit balances in a customer's account(s) may be offset by any other outstanding balance owed by or to the customer. Please allow 4 to 6 weeks for delivery. Offer available while quantities last.

Your Privacy—The Reader Service is committed to protecting your privacy. Our Privacy Policy is available online at www.ReaderService.com or upon request from the Reader Service.

We make a portion of our mailing list available to reputable third parties that offer products we believe may interest you. If you prefer that we not exchange your name with third parties, or if you wish to clarify or modify your communication preferences, please visit us at www.ReaderService.com/consumerchoice or write to us at Reader Service Preference Service, P.O. Box 9062, Buffalo, NY 14269. Include your complete name and address.

HRI1B

Harlequin® Special Edition® is thrilled to present a new installment in USA TODAY bestselling author RaeAnne Thayne's reader-favorite miniseries, THE COWBOYS OF COLD CREEK.

Join the excitement as we meet the Bowmans—four siblings who lost their parents but keep family ties alive in Pine Gulch. First up is Trace. Only two things get under this rugged lawman's skin: beautiful women and secrets. And in Rebecca Parsons, he finds both!

Read on for a sneak peek of CHRISTMAS IN COLD CREEK. Available November 2011 from Harlequin® Special Edition®.

On impulse, he unfolded himself from the bar stool. "Need a hand?"

"Thank you! I…" She lifted her gaze from the floor to his jeans and then raised her eyes. When she identified him her hazel eyes turned from grateful to unfriendly and cold, as if he'd somehow thrown the broken glasses at her head.

He also thought he saw a glimmer of panic in those interesting depths, which instantly stirred his curiosity like cream swirling through coffee.

"I've got it, Officer. Thank you." Her voice was several degrees colder than the whirl of sleet outside the windows.

Despite her protests, he knelt down beside her and began to pick up shards of broken glass. "No problem. Those trays can be slippery."

This close, he picked up the scent of her, something fresh and flowery that made him think of a mountain meadow on a July afternoon. She had a soft, lush mouth and for one brief, insane moment, he wanted to push aside that stray lock of hair slipping from her ponytail and taste her. Apparently he needed to spend a lot less time working and a great deal *more* time recreating with the opposite sex if he could have sudden random fantasies about a woman he wasn't even inclined to like, pretty or not.

"I'm Trace Bowman. You must be new in town."

She didn't answer immediately and he could almost see the wheels turning in her head. Why the hesitancy? And why that little hint of unease he could see clouding the edge of her gaze? His presence was obviously making her uncomfortable and Trace couldn't help wondering why.

"Yes. We've been here a few weeks."

"Well, I'm just up the road about four lots, in the white house with the cedar shake roof, if you or your daughter need anything." He smiled at her as he picked up the last shard of glass and set it on her tray.

Definitely a story there, he thought as she hurried away. He just might need to dig a little into her background to find out why someone with fine clothes and nice jewelry, and who so obviously didn't have experience as a waitress, would be here slinging hash at The Gulch. Was she running away from someone? A bad marriage?

So…Rebecca Parsons. Not Becky. An intriguing woman. It had been a long time since one of those had crossed his path here in Pine Gulch.

Trace won't rest until he finds out Rebecca's secret, but will he still have that same attraction to her once he does? Find out in CHRISTMAS IN COLD CREEK. Available November 2011 from Harlequin® Special Edition®.

brings you

USA TODAY Bestselling Author

Penny Jordan

Part of the new miniseries

RUSSIAN RIVALS

*Demidov vs. Androvonov—let the most
merciless of men win...*

Kiryl Androvonov

The Russian oligarch has one rival: billionaire
Vasilii Demidov. Luckily, Vasilii has an Achilles' heel—his
younger, overprotected, beautiful half sister, Alena...

Vasilii Demidov

After losing his sister to his bitter rival, Vasilii is far too
cynical to ever trust a woman, not even his secretary Laura.
Never did she expect to be at the ruthless Russian's mercy....

The rivalry begins in...

THE MOST COVETED PRIZE—November
THE POWER OF VASILII—December

Available wherever
Harlequin Presents® books are sold.

www.Harlequin.com

HP13023

Harlequin
Super Romance

Discover a fresh, heartfelt new romance
from acclaimed author

Sarah Mayberry

Businessman Flynn Randall's life is
complicated. So he doesn't need the
distraction of fun, spontaneous Mel Porter.
But he can't stop thinking about her. Maybe
he can handle one more complication....

All They Need

LONGER
BOOK
Same Price!

*Available November 8, 2011,
wherever books are sold!*